KRISTI HELVIG

STRANGE SKIES

BURN OUT BOOK TWO

• • • • •

EGMONT
Publishing
NEW YORK

EGMONT

We bring stories to life

First published by Egmont Publishing, 2015
443 Park Avenue South, Suite 806
New York, NY 10016

Copyright © Kristi Helvig, 2015
All rights reserved

1 3 5 7 9 8 6 4 2

www.egmontusa.com
www.kristihelvig.com

Library of Congress Cataloging-in-Publication Data
Helvig, Kristi.
Strange skies / Kristi Helvig.
pages cm. -- (Burn out ; book 2)
Summary: Tora Reynolds has escaped to a new planet, but must fight against the
Consulate and a rebel leader to find and destroy her father's guns.
ISBN 978-1-60684-481-6 (hardcover)
ISBN 978-1-60684-482-3 (eBook)
[1. Survival--Fiction. 2. Government, Resistance to--Fiction. 3. Weapons--Fiction.
4. Mercenary troops--Fiction. 5. Orphans--Fiction. 6. Science fiction.] I. Title.
PZ7.H37623Str 2015
[Fic]--dc23
2014018573

Printed in the United States of America

• • •

For Mom
For everything

• • •

• • •

When it is dark enough, you can see the stars.

• • •

Chapter ONE

Three Months Later

THE BOY FACED AWAY FROM ME, LOOKING AT SOMETHING IN the distance. His profile showed off short blond hair cut in a military style, which contrasted with the stubble across his jaw. Something about him was familiar and made my heart race. I looked down to find he was holding my hand, and I felt both terrified and safe. A loud sound echoed nearby and he turned toward me. That's when I saw the gun in his hand. Fear caused my throat to tighten as his eyes locked with mine.

"Hurry, run. Come with me," he said. The inflection in his voice made the words sound like a plea.

My eyes flew open and the dream dissipated. Sweat drenched my body and my teeth chattered. I struggled to pull up the blanket but it, too, was soaked. Pain racked my head as I tried to figure out where the hell I was. Judging by the temperature, I was being held in a giant icebox.

When I attempted to sit up, my arms refused to support my weight. My eyes fell on a small device near my right hand, and I summoned all my energy to press its red button. The pounding in my head competed with widespread chills.

A high-pitched beeping of a nearby monitor permeated my consciousness. Goose bumps broke out on my arms as my skin registered the cold air. An extra thin blanket lay on the cot by my feet, yet I couldn't find the strength to pull it up. My eyes had trouble focusing, and I could just make out the gigantic form coming toward me. A mix of relief and hostility swirled through my brain. I couldn't think straight. I didn't know what it meant.

"Morning, Miss Sunshine," the large woman grumbled. "Couldn't even wait another hour for your dose, could you?"

I stared back at the red button under my finger. So I'd caused the beeping sound. The woman grabbed my arm as though she expected resistance, but my limb was limp in her hand. Her dark eyes bored into me as she lifted a green med tube and pressed the tip of it to my arm. I swear she smirked as she pressed the injection trigger.

Instant warmth flooded my veins and my body relaxed. Everything felt right with the world again. Something small nagged at the back of my mind—something I was supposed to do, or remember—but the meds quickly swept the troubled thoughts away. A familiar deep heaviness settled in and my eyelids drooped. Utter bliss and peace filled me, and I yawned as the woman retreated wordlessly from the room. I couldn't remember my own name if my life depended on it, not that it mattered. I felt great. I could stay here forever.

A deep voice echoed throughout the room as I drifted in and out of consciousness. I didn't see anyone, so maybe I was hallucinating. The voice said the same things over and over again. *The Consulate serves. The Consulate protects. The Consulate's weapons help us to protect you. The Consulate is your friend.*

Every once in a while I'd stir awake and swear someone was in the room with me. I caught the scent of wildflowers a few times, yet when I opened my eyes, the room was empty. I drifted back into sleep but couldn't shake the feeling that I wasn't really alone.

I tried to clear my thoughts but whatever meds the woman gave me made my brain feel like mush. I remembered being injured and aboard a ship. A Consulate ship. The Consulate must have saved me from something and brought me here. Was this Caelia?

The Consulate is your friend.

I stared up at the faceless voice. The Consulate must be helping me to get better. *Then why is that woman so unpleasant? And why can't I remember anything?*

A brief scan around the windowless room provided

little in the way of clues. The walls were definitely not those of a ship. The sparse furniture consisted only of the ramshackle cot I occupied and a rickety bedside table that tottered on three legs. I shifted on the bed and felt the tube between my legs. I stared in horror at the urine-filled bag that it led to. The fact that I couldn't piss on my own meant I must be really sick.

Push the button. My finger inched toward the device. Pushing the button would end the headache and icy cold. The large woman would help me. She'd give me medicine to make me feel better. My hand trembled as it touched the button, but I hesitated. Disjointed thoughts raced through my brain. Even scarier than not knowing where I was, was not knowing *who* I was.

The deep voice started in again from above. *The Consulate serves. The Consulate protects. The Consulate weapons help us to protect you. The Consulate is your friend.* I stared at the ceiling and noticed a small device where the voice seemed to be coming from. It stopped suddenly as the sound of footsteps reached my door, followed by hushed voices. I allowed myself to slide back against the pillow and closed my eyes as the door opened. More footsteps came to the side of my bed.

"She's an hour past her dose but hasn't pushed the button. What do you think, doctor?" It was the large woman who had given me the injection of amazing medicine.

Just open your eyes and she'll give it to you. Your pain will disappear. I tried to ignore the voice in my head.

"She's still out cold and I don't want an accidental overdose. She's no good to us dead." An image of spectacles and a shiny coat popped into my head, but disappeared again. He must be one of the doctors treating my illness, whatever it was. But what did he mean by overdose?

He felt my pulse and scanned me with something that caused a warm buzzing over my body. I wanted them to leave. The doctor's hand rested on my arm and a chill went down my spine. He cleared his throat. "Are you awake?"

I pretended to stir. "Mmmm."

"It's Dr. Sorokin. How are you feeling?"

It took so much effort to form words. "I'm not sure. What's wrong with me? Where am I?"

Dr. Sorokin glanced at the woman before answering me with a question of his own. "What do you remember?"

I focused my thoughts but it was all a hazy blur. "All I remember is a Consulate ship but I don't remember why I was there. I think I was hurt. Why can't I remember anything?"

Dr. Sorokin smiled at the woman. The look on his face was smug, almost triumphant. I didn't like it. "Yes, you were injured. Sometimes trauma can cause memory loss, so I wouldn't worry too much about it. You are safe now— you're in a Consulate center on Caelia, the new Earth." He studied my face, as though waiting for a reaction. "How do you feel about the Consulate?"

I knew the word *Consulate* meant something to me, but all I could recall was what I'd heard from the ceiling. I struggled to speak again. "Are they the ones who gave me these meds?"

Dr. Sorokin's hand was icy on my arm. I wanted to pull away but didn't have the strength. "Yes, the Consulate is giving you medicine to help you get better."

I started to drift off again but fought it. "Then I think they're fabulous. I love the Consulate." My eyes fluttered shut, and I hoped they'd think I had fallen back asleep. All I wanted was this man to take his cold hand off my body.

He shook my arm but I played dead. Dr. Sorokin sighed and spoke to the woman. "Give her two more hours, max, then wake her. Allan thinks we can safely begin Phase Two. We started too early last time. These drugs should have erased a lot of her memories by now, and she's so dependent on them that she'll do whatever we want to get more. We have her just where we want her."

The woman chuckled. "Heard her mother was an addict too. Guess we don't need to worry about this one running away again."

They left the room. My brain tried—and failed—to compute what I'd just heard. I had run away from these people? That meant I was a prisoner. I could barely manage to push a button, yet somehow I had attempted to escape this place. And they'd said I was dependent on drugs. That explained why I craved the meds so badly. But the woman's comment stuck with me. She'd said my mother was an addict too. *Mother? Where was my mother?*

I fought off sleep as another wave of exhaustion

crashed into me. Whatever Dr. Sorokin had in store for me wasn't good—I knew that much. The haze started to confuse my brain again, but I pushed through the fog to search for memories. Fractured images swirled, then slowly merged in my mind. Images of a fiery red sun, an army of guns, a boy with blond stubble and a sandpaper voice, a father bent over a notebook, and last, a little girl in a pale flowered shirt. My eyes widened in shock as the pictures crystallized. It took all of my strength to lift my hand and wipe the beads of sweat from my forehead. I opened my mouth and my voice was still weak and scratchy, but I heard myself clearly.

"I am Tora Reynolds."

Though I had no clue how long I'd been held captive, all that mattered was the two short hours I had left before Dr. Sorokin and Nurse Nasty came back for me. It was still hard to comprehend that after refusing meds my entire life, I'd become an even worse addict than my mother. Against my will but an addict nonetheless.

A fresh batch of sweat poured from my skin, and the throbbing in my head resumed. Was it more sad or funny that though I wanted to escape, I couldn't help but feel that a "tiny dose" of meds would help the process go more smoothly?

I surveyed my attire and sighed. The only thing on me was a thermoplastic gown, presumably for easier access to the catheter tubing. That would have to go first. I took a deep breath and pulled out the long, thin tube. I winced as it slid out, mentally filed the task under "Things I Never Want to Do Again."

Then I leaned over and checked the drawer in the bedside table, but it was empty. I had a vague recollection of my satchel but it was nowhere in sight. Guess I'd have to make do with the gown. Not that I had much chance of blending in, anyway, with my shaking hands and sweat-drenched hair. The door seemed incredibly far away as I swung my legs to the floor.

I took an unsteady step and had to lean on the table for support. I tried again and made it two whole steps before my knees buckled and I fell. It was like I was learning to walk all over again. My fingers brushed the cold tile and I inhaled deeply. *You can do this,* I told myself. *Yeah, but wouldn't it be easier with a little help of the chemical variety?* I gritted my teeth. At this rate it would take the whole two hours just to make it to the door. I pushed up from the floor. After what felt like a million shaky steps, I reached it and leaned my head against the cold surface.

No footsteps sounded outside so I reached for the door handle with bated breath. There was no energetic lock that I could see. It was open. Guess being in a vegetative state for so long had lulled these people into a false sense of security. Good thing, because if it had been locked, I think I would have laid down right there and taken a nap.

The door opened easily, but it still took a crazy amount of effort on my part. How in the hell was I going to escape if opening a door was problematic? The hallway was clear, but I had no idea which way to go. It wasn't like they had the flashing exit signs that had lined the halls of Dad's Consulate building job. Dad's Consulate job. A whole new host of memories flooded back, and I pushed them away for the time being. I needed to get out of this place first.

My room was around the center point of the hallway, and it stretched about thirty feet on either side. There were no windows. One direction looked to be a few feet shorter than the other, so I headed that way. It was just as cold in the hall as in my room. Only a few dim lights hung from makeshift holders on the wall.

The entire building looked primitive in construction, consisting of a dark brown material I'd never seen before. Still, it was an actual building, which meant I'd probably been here awhile. It had to have been several months since I'd been picked up by the Consulate ship. Several months since I'd tried to keep my dad's bioenergetic weapons out of enemy hands and failed miserably. Guns that only I— and apparently James—could fire. Several months since Kale had landed on that crazy-ass shifting planet, watched James shoot me, and then took off with the guns when the Consulate descended. I saw the lasers from the soldiers' guns tear into James right before I'd detonated T.O., the most powerful bomb ever made.

James. The name sent shivers down my spine. When the shivers increased to the point of shaking, I realized that withdrawal, rather than conflicted feelings, was the culprit. My limbs twitched uncontrollably, and I broke out in a sweat yet again. The urge to vomit was overwhelming.

It was impossible that my skin felt so hot, but I was so cold, like an icy fire ran through my veins instead of blood. *Ticktock*. I'd killed at least thirty minutes already and was getting nowhere fast. My long-term plan of finding Kale and the guns was toast if my short-term goal of walking didn't go so well. I pushed myself to take several more steps. There were no other doors in this hallway. I made it to the corner and turned. This corridor was shorter, only about twenty feet long and ended at a door.

About fifteen feet away from me on the right was another door, but it was the end of the hallway that made my heart skip. Faint light shone from behind it. It had to be an exit. I hobbled along as quickly as possible. The cold feeling had entirely disappeared. In fact, it felt downright toasty. Maybe this was a lull in the withdrawal symptoms. I hoped so because I'd sweated out most of the liquid in my body and would kill for some Caelia Pure.

I'd gotten about halfway down the hall when I heard a noise from somewhere behind me. I turned around but saw nothing there. As I took another step, other sounds became clearer—footsteps and voices. It was the large woman and someone else. Not the doctor, but the person sounded vaguely familiar.

They had to be heading toward my room. The sound of a door opening followed by the woman's loud, panicked voice confirmed it. No way had it been two hours, had it?

Crap. I attempted to run to the exit, but it ended up being more like a drunken shuffle. I'd never make it.

The door on my right-hand side was only a foot away. It didn't have a lock either and was my only shot. They would turn the corner in a second and see me. I lurched for the door. Inside, I shut it and pressed my back against it to keep them out. My legs were rubbery and I knew I couldn't hold on for much longer. I was out of juice.

I leaned my head back and looked around the room. It was identical to mine, down to the bed and table. Down to a figure lying comatose in the center of the bed, though the person, at least, had managed to pull the covers up around him. Curious about my fellow prisoner, I stepped toward the bed. It wasn't like I had the strength to keep anyone out of the room anyway.

The blanket covered most of his face but his forehead was covered in sweat. At least I assumed it was a "he" due to the short gray hair. It must be close to his next dose time too. The building's cooling system must have been out of whack—unless they were using a bizarre method of torture by climate control. I reached out and tugged the cover down. *Holy mother of god.*

I couldn't even comprehend what I was seeing. Maybe it was a hallucination from the drugs. His eyes widened in shock and confusion that must have mirrored my own.

"Tora? Is that you?" his voice croaked.

I touched his face to make sure it was real.

"Yes. Yes, Dad. It's me."

Chapter TWO

DAD REACHED FOR MY WRIST AND ATTEMPTED TO SIT UP. His hand was frail and bony. I helped pull him to a seated position and placed a pillow behind him so he could lean back. He struggled to speak. "They told me you were dead. All this time, I thought you were dead."

I squeezed his hand. "They told me the same thing about you." The fact that he sat here in front of me still wasn't totally registering. I think it was a combination of shock and the drugs.

His sunken eyes were so different from the calm, confident gaze I remembered. He'd glance up from his notebooks to wave me into his study, and I'd curl up to read on the bench in his room while he worked, always feeling safe when he was near. Now, he didn't look like he could protect himself, let alone anyone else. "What have they done to you, Dad? Have they had you all this time?"

"Ever since that so-called meeting back on Earth. I should have known it was a trap. They said they'd let me go as soon as I told them where the guns were. Later, they claimed they'd found the guns and that you were dead, so I might as well work with them." His voice broke. "I still wouldn't cooperate, so after they transported me to Caelia, they started experimenting with various drugs. Drugs to make me compliant." He coughed. "I guess I'm still not very compliant, though."

"Like father, like daughter." I patted his arm. "They gave me different drugs too. Ones to make me forget. They thought if I lost my memories, I'd forget what burners they were."

I remembered the last page of Mom's journal, the one where Dad had written about how I'd locked Callie out of the bunker. How Callie had died and then Mom sank next to her by the boulder and let herself burn alive right outside our shelter door. A torrent of emotions overcame me. Guilt. Grief. Relief.

The reality of Dad being alive finally hit me, and I threw my arms around him. All those lonely nights after he never returned from that meeting when I thought he'd been killed. A sob tore from my throat. "I'm so sorry about Mom and Callie," I said. "I read the journal. I never meant—"

"Shhh," said Dad. "That's not important now. What matters is that you're okay." Tears leaked from his eyes. "I can't believe you're sitting here in front of me."

"We can't stay here long. They'll find us. We need to get you out of here." I glanced around the room and back at Dad, who didn't look strong enough to walk ten feet. Not that I was in much better shape.

The reunion was short-lived. The door flew open, banging against the wall. I stared openmouthed at the person standing next to the woman. Alec. The guy from Sector 2 who I'd talked Markus into rescuing back on Earth. How was this possible? The heavyset woman gasped for air, red-faced as she bent over with her hand to her chest. I might have a slight chance in hell of getting by her, but I'd never get by Alec.

Alec stared at me calmly as he spoke. "Tora Reynolds, you have violated Consulate Code 5223 by attempting to leave the premises."

I wanted to kick myself for ever buying his act about being an abandoned survivor, though the dog thing was a nice touch. Where was Lucy? I should have saved the dog and left him to rot.

"Really? Is there a code for kidnapping and drugging innocent people, 'cause I'm pretty sure you're in violation of that one." I no longer considered his accent cute. My legs wobbled underneath me and I had to sit on the edge of Dad's bed.

The large woman finally found her breath, along with her evil smile. "I believe you know Lieutenant Colonel Alec Hayes. He was instrumental in helping us to locate you on Earth."

If I'd had an ounce of strength left, I would've launched myself at him and torn his eyes out. Instead, I glared with all the venom I could muster, which probably looked plain pitiful given my current condition. "You freakin' burner."

Alec stared back without bothering to respond. The woman pulled a syringe from her pocket and handed it to him. "You can do the honors."

She smirked at me. "You will never, ever run away again. I'll see to that." Spit flew from her mouth and I pretended to wipe my cheek.

Alec came toward me and spun the syringe in his hand like he was playing with it. He wasn't just following orders—he seemed to be enjoying himself. I hoped he injected himself by accident.

I let loose a string of every expletive I could think of but my words were hollow, and I couldn't back them up with action. My legs were done. They felt like jelly against the bed.

"Please don't do this." Dad put his hand up weakly in Alec's direction. "I'll do whatever you want, but don't hurt Tora."

The woman's lips curled back, revealing yellowed teeth. "You promised that before, remember? You don't follow through so well."

Alec reached my side.

"It's okay, Dad." I gave his arm an awkward hug. "I've made it this far. I'll get you out of here, I promise."

The woman laughed. "Over my dead body."

I shrugged at her. "Have it your way."

Alec pulled my arm out roughly. Tears pricked my eyes. Why was he doing this? He placed the syringe against the place where my bicep muscle used to be and pressed the button.

Everything swam before my eyes and then went dark. As I hit the floor, it dawned on me that though Alec had been holding my arm, he didn't even try to break my fall.

James sat next to me on a cot. I looked past him toward the door. We were in my room in the containment center, and I knew we had to be careful. Someone wanted to hurt us. His hazel-green eyes stared into mine. "Please," he said, then his lips were on mine. My body responded though my brain screamed for me to stop. His hands moved slowly down my arms. Then he tightened his grip. I tried to pull away but he wouldn't let go. He started shaking me.

I gradually came out of the dream but couldn't fully wake. The shaking didn't stop. It wasn't just my arms. My entire body quaked. Great. *More withdrawal symptoms.* I didn't want to open my eyes. Maybe I could sleep through it. I tried to slip back into unconsciousness. The spasms continued. From a faraway place, someone called my name. Finally, I realized that I wasn't shaking—someone was shaking me.

I fought the urge to wake up.

"Dammit, open your eyes!"

He didn't have to be so rude about it. It took tremendous effort, but my eyelids cracked open to slits. "What? I'm trying to sleep here," I mumbled. My eyes crashed shut again.

Cold water sprayed my face and my eyes flew open. *Alec.* I swung my fist at him but he easily caught my hand. "Knock it off, Tora. We have to go."

I blinked. "I'm not going anywhere with you."

Alec sighed as though I was acting like a petulant child. "I didn't give you the dose. I switched the syringe with another one I had in my pocket." He pulled on my arm.

I twisted out of his grasp with what little strength I had. "Do you think I'm stupid? If you didn't give me the dose, then why have I slept like the dead for hours?"

He pulled out a pair of cotton pants and a T-shirt from a bag. "Not hours, *ángel.* Minutes. I gave you a quick-acting sleep agent, but had to make it look real." He tossed the clothes at me. "We don't have much time before Sylvia comes back."

"You must be referring to the big-boned bee-atch."

Alec nodded. "There's a med to help with the withdrawal symptoms but Sylvia must have moved it. I didn't have time to keep looking."

I fingered the pants and frowned. "Wait, these are *my* pants."

"Yes, from your things in storage." He gestured for me to hurry.

Something about having my own pants made me

insanely happy. I picked up the white T-shirt. "But this isn't mine . . . it's way too big—" No way. I held the shirt to my nose and inhaled. The scent of him was faint, but still there. *Because what could be more romantic than wearing the shirt of the guy who shot you?*

Now Alec looked impatient. "I don't know what to tell you, but it was with your stuff. Can we please leave now?" He tossed me my satchel with the rest of my things. Callie's wildflower painting was there. I resisted the urge to pull it out and nodded at him.

Alec waited outside while I changed. The T-shirt hung loosely over my pants—I had to admit it was comfy. My legs were still weak, but the thought of getting out of this place propelled me to the door.

Alec glanced down the hallway and motioned me forward.

I sniffed. "Just because I'm coming with you doesn't mean you don't have a lot of explaining to do."

He placed his hand under my elbow to support me. "Don't worry. We'll have plenty of time for that."

Dad's door was just ahead. He was in much worse shape than I was—probably because he'd been imprisoned longer. I hoped he could at least walk. I slowed as we neared his room.

Alec shook his head. "Tora—"

"I'm not leaving without him." I opened the door to an empty room. The cot was stripped bare, no evidence that it had ever been occupied by my only living family member. I swiveled to face Alec. "Where is he?"

He tugged on my arm to pull me toward the exit. "He's fine. They moved him somewhere else. They didn't want to chance another escape attempt. They figured you'd try to take him with you."

I pulled my arm back. "Then we need to find him."

Alec sighed. "We will, but not now. I don't know exactly where he is, but I do know that we're almost out of time. We'll come back, but you can't help your dad if you're caught again."

Alec had a point. I watched him pull a small metal object from his shirt when we reached the final door.

"What is that?"

"It's a key from an old-school lock on Earth. The Consulate brought a bunch of this stuff from the archives building to hold them over until they got their technology up and running."

I thought of my dad's high-tech guns and wondered if they were still in Kale's possession. Alec slid the key into the lock on the door and turned it. "I think they had a bit of a shock coming here. They had all the Earth money they could ever want, which didn't mean anything once they landed. Everyone went back to survival mode."

The door opened and Alec stepped outside. "Wait!" I shrieked. "Don't we need suits?"

Alec put his finger to his lips to shush me but showed a

hint of a smile. "Nope. There's plenty of air on Caelia and the sun is, well, it's different. Come on."

I took a hesitant step out into the daylight. The sun was a gold color, much smaller than the huge red inferno that had ruled Earth. I stretched out my bare arm and the sunlight warmed my skin. Memories of blisters popping out on my hands, of Mom and Callie burning alive, reared up to haunt me. I tried in vain to pull my short sleeves down for cover. "My arm. It feels hot."

Alec grabbed my arm and urged me onward. "You're fine. It's not going to burn. Have I mentioned we need to get out of here?"

I willed my legs to cooperate, but their plans favored sitting and resting. I hung on to Alec and stared down at my legs as though I could make them remain upright with the power of my gaze.

"Come on, hurry," Alec said. "We just need to make it to the tree line."

"The tree what?" I looked up from my feet and gasped. Trees. Real trees as far as the eye could see. We were in a clearing in the midst of a ton of huge, leafy, green trees. It was a far cry from the deadly, sharp cactus groves on Earth. I struggled to recall the word I'd seen on my Infinity and gestured at the friendly-looking foliage. "What's this called again?"

Alec smiled but didn't stop tugging at me. "It's a forest."

I tried it out. "Forest." The word sounded beautiful on my tongue. "It's my new favorite word."

"I think there's a word you'll like even better, but we'll never get there if the Consulate catches us."

As though on cue, loud shouts echoed from inside the building we'd escaped. "Guess Sylvia just figured out I'm missing . . . again," I said.

My legs churned sluggishly beneath me, but I was determined to get to the forest. It killed me that I had to leave my dad so soon after discovering he wasn't dead. *Sorry Dad,* I thought. *I'll be back for you as soon as I can.* I would get him out of there somehow, and the Consulate was going to pay for what they'd done to him.

Alec didn't let go of my arm. My feet tripped over themselves as I tried to keep up.

We hit the tree line just as the building door opened. Alec pulled me behind a large tree and we looked into the clearing. Sylvia was bent at the knees and looked as though she was about to throw up. Next to her was the shiny-coated, fake-glasses-wearing Dr. Sorokin, who had treated me on the Consulate ship. He turned around in a slow circle, peering into the trees that surrounded the building.

I stared at the ugly, bleak building in the center of the lush forest. They'd obviously cut down some of the trees to make room for their makeshift prison. Leave it to the Consulate—they'd found an amazing, beautiful planet and had already started to wreck it.

After a minute, Dr. Sorokin reached into his pocket and pulled out a tele-com device.

Alec tugged at my sleeve. "He's calling for Consulate backup. We have to go," he whispered.

Cold sweats, fatigue, and nausea warred for control of my body. Though another visit with the shiny coats was the last thing I wanted, I was pretty positive I couldn't move another step.

"Where are we going?" I asked, swaying.

Alec's eyes bored into mine as he steadied me. "Somewhere I know you'll want to see. Callie City."

Chapter THREE

My sister's name perked me up. Dr. Sorokin had mentioned Callie City back on the Consulate ship. Just after I had awakened, he'd told me that my rescuer, a.k.a. James, had said Dad's guns would be found in Callie City—a place named after my dead sister. A city that couldn't have even existed at the time, since I'd only just told James her name. I didn't know why James had made up such a blatant lie—not that he'd ever win any honesty awards—but maybe that meant I'd find James there and could get some answers. I'd start with why he shot me, and where my dad's guns were.

"What's Callie City?" I asked, feigning ignorance as I wiped a fresh batch of sweat from my forehead.

"A Resistance settlement set up to fight the Consulate. James named it." Alec gripped my arm. "Now no more questions until we're out of here. Let's move."

I straightened up as best I could. "Okay, let's do this."

We headed deeper into the forest. Despite my cold sweats, I stared in awe at the towering trees around me. All I'd known for years was the confined, underground bunker my dad had built. Before that, I'd lived under a dome and never seen any live thing except other humans and some mutant cacti. Even though I'd seen pictures of plants and animals on the Infinity, it was hard to believe those things had really existed. I reached up to touch one of the green leaves. It was smooth and soft under my fingertips. Brightly colored winged creatures, smaller than the birds I'd seen on the Net, zipped to and fro, making a strange musical sound. They didn't seem bothered by us at all. The air smelled sweet and clean. "Do you even realize how amazing this is? We're breathing air. Outside. Without helmets."

Alec tugged at my arm. "You wouldn't even believe all the things I've seen here. But if we don't hurry, all *you'll* see is the containment building again."

Sure enough, a ship roared overhead not far from us.

"Looks like the backup is here," Alec said. He raced ahead about ten steps and craned his neck toward the sky. "The ship shouldn't be able to spot us if we stay in the trees and the land cruisers are too big to navigate in here. Our problem will be the ground units they're probably dispatching right now."

I grunted. "Yeah, guess you'd know all about their tactics, since you're Consulate. Weren't you going to explain about all that?"

He slowed his pace and linked his arm with mine. "I promise to tell you everything when we're safe. It might not seem like it, but I've never lied to you, *ángel*."

I ignored the term of endearment. "Lies of omission are still lies." I left my arm in his only because I wasn't sure how many more steps I could handle on my own. Sweat ran down from my hairline into my eyes, and I wiped at my face with my free hand. My body screamed in pain. I would have done almost anything for another dose of meds.

Alec ignored my comment as he half-carried, half-pulled me through the forest. "I don't hear the ship," he said.

"So?"

"So they've probably landed to send ground units after us."

Fabulous. I was barely faster than the trees, and they were standing still. I couldn't outrun soldiers. My breath came out in ragged gasps. "This is the part where you tell me you have a plan, preferably one involving transportation. I can't walk much farther."

Alec's voice remained calm. "*Lo siento,* no transport, but there's a place we can hide. I scouted ahead of time to be safe."

My vision was starting to blur. No weapons seemed a bigger problem than transportation at the moment. Alec had only one standard-issue gun holstered to his side. The Consulate guys would have more ammo than that. "Is that your only weapon?" I asked.

He shifted the small pack on his back, raised his arm, and flexed his biceps. "Not if you count these babies."

His arms actually looked quite strong, which was good since everything around me was starting to fade. "I do count those," I said, stumbling again. "In fact, I think you're going to need them right about now." I closed my eyes as the world went black.

Everything was dark and still. I sat up in the inky blackness. "Alec?" I whispered.

No response. My heart sped up at the thought of being alone in a strange place. I reached out and felt a cool, damp wall. The texture of it was similar to the large boulders that had been outside our underground bunker on Earth. Just like the one my mom and sister had died beside. My fingers brushed my satchel. I took a deep breath, hoisted the bag over my shoulder, and stood up. My legs still felt weak but the cold sweats had subsided.

My eyes tried to adjust to the dark, but everything remained black. I stretched my arms above me and my fingertips hit a ceiling that felt like it was made of rock. I took a few tentative steps with my arm reached out ahead until I hit a wall in front of me. *Was I inside a giant rock?* I moved slowly and ran my hand along the damp stone as I went.

After a few minutes going in the same direction, the darkness ahead lightened a bit. I walked faster and relief flooded through me. My legs felt a little stronger with each step. As I neared the area where faint light was visible, a cool breeze brushed my face. The scent of something heavenly wafted through the air.

I reached the end and exited the stone structure. It was night but there were no lethal storms. The breeze was gentle, no threat of destruction beneath its soft currents. I turned back to examine where I'd been. It looked like a huge rock that had been hollowed out. A vague recollection of something I'd seen on the GlobalNet surfaced but I couldn't pull up the memory.

I tossed my hair back and let the ripples of wind sweep through it. What I saw above me took my breath away. The light I'd noticed came from what looked like thousands of twinkling stars. They blinked and sparkled like a carpet of diamonds had been rolled out across the sky. Not one, but two luminous moons stood watch among them. I'd never seen anything so strange and beautiful.

An arm grabbed me from behind.

I screamed as a hand clamped over my mouth.

"Shhh. It's just me. Alec."

My body relaxed. "You shouldn't sneak up on people like that."

Alec came around to stand at my side, his gun in his hand. He spoke in a low voice. "Good to see you awake and well. You crashed hard. I've been keeping watch outside the cave while you slept."

Cave. *That's what it was.*

"Any sign of them?" I asked.

Alec tucked the gun back into his holster. "They came

close about an hour ago but they moved on. They're way ahead of us now, which works in our favor."

I stretch again, loving the feel of the delicious air. "How long have I been out?"

"Just a few hours."

I frowned. "Then how is it night already?"

"It's not like Earth. Night and day cycle much faster here . . . every four hours instead of every twenty-four, so we just say light breaks and dark breaks."

My head couldn't wrap itself around the concept. "So, there are like eighteen hundred some days in a year? Or does that mean there aren't years the way we think of them?"

Alec shrugged. "I'm not sure time matters like it did before. At least not in the same way." He pointed at the two moons. "*Loco,* huh?"

"Huh, it's gonna take some getting used to." I stared at the small glowing orbs. "Pretty, though."

"I'll say." Alec's face was turned toward me. He looked back up at the sky. "See those stars right there, the two bright ones? One of them has a trail of smaller stars underneath, and the other stars surround all of them in a circle shape."

I squinted. "Yeah, I see them."

"They remind me of a face, the bright stars are the eyes and the smaller ones are the tears. I call it the 'Weeping Boy.' It's cool being on a new planet—you can name any constellation you want."

Dad had once told me about the constellations on Earth, but I'd had to satisfy myself with seeing them on the Infinity since it wasn't safe to go outside at night. Once Kale and his soldiers came along, we had ventured out a few times after dark in order to outsmart the Consulate, but I'd been too busy running to notice the sky.

I stared at the Weeping Boy a second longer, then met Alec's gaze. "That's fascinating, really. But I want you to explain yourself and how you were working for the Consulate, right after you tell me that Lucy and Markus are okay."

Alec's tone was serious. "Lucy's good. James is taking care of her."

Hearing his name on someone else's lips made my heart skip. "James?" He didn't strike me as a dog person. "What about Markus? And how did James get to Callie City anyway? He was on the Consulate ship with me."

Alec coughed and I knew he was weighing his words. "I better let James tell his side of the story. As for Markus, well, he didn't want anything to do with Lucy."

That was an understatement. I remembered how he resented Britta fawning all over the dog. But still, it was weird that he wouldn't help out.

Alec flashed the illuminated screen of his com device toward me in the dark. "This one is recent. James has been good about sending pics even though I don't think he likes me much."

Lucy was crouched down with her head toward the

floor and her butt in the air, tail wagging behind her. She looked at the camera like she was ready to pounce on the photographer and lick him to death. I wished James was in the picture too, but he wasn't exactly the type to snap photos of himself.

I smiled. "She looks great. You must be excited to see her again."

"Yeah, which reminds me, we gotta keep moving. Our contact is meeting us at the next light break."

"Light break," I repeated. It sounded weird, but I guess the terms *night* and *day* weren't really accurate anymore.

Alec pulled an energy packet from the pack slung over his shoulder and handed it to me. I drank as we walked through the trees. We used the starlight that managed to penetrate the forest to guide us. Every once in a while, the drone of a ship sounded overhead and a bright light would sweep the area. I doubted they could see more than the tops of trees in the dark, but still froze in place until they passed.

The energy packet worked wonders. It had been a long time since I'd had anything other than meds and intravenous fluids. I felt stronger than I had in a long time. Alec handed me a bottle of Caelia Pure and I gulped it down in three sips. Chills still occasionally racked my body, but I'd take that over being drugged up again in a heartbeat. This new world was breathtaking.

I wiped my mouth with the sleeve of my shirt. "Okay, Alec. Start talking."

He moved fast and I tried to keep up. "There's really not much to tell. I was Consulate . . . long before I met you. Once I figured out they weren't the good guys, I stepped back, but you can't just quit the Consulate. They'd kill you."

"So, so . . ." I panted and wheezed. I might not have cold sweats anymore but lying on my ass in a containment cell hadn't done wonders for my cardio. That reminded me of James running shirtless on Dad's motion machine. I shook my head. "So, the Consulate didn't know you weren't working for them anymore?"

"Right. That day I hid from under my friend's pod wasn't because I thought the Consulate would kill me. It was because I knew they'd make me kill others," he whispered, anger seething through his words.

He stomped ahead. "It worked out, though. I'd been in the Resistance settlement, now called Callie City, for about three weeks after Kale dropped Markus and me off, when we heard you were taken to the containment center in Consulate City. I went there and acted like I'd been kidnapped by the Resistance while on Earth. I fed them some fake intel so they'd trust me. Even did this to myself." He pointed to a scar across his cheek. "Told them I got it when I tried to get away, and that I killed the Resistance soldiers who'd taken me. The Consulate congratulated me on my dedication and put me to work right away."

The stars became less visible as the sky lightened. I glared at Alec in the twilight, or dawn, or whatever it was called now. "Back up. On Earth, you didn't tell me the whole Consulate bit. Why?"

Alec looked at me sideways. "Right. Because you still would have come to rescue me if you knew I was Consulate, but not really?"

I thought about it. "Probably not. Trust isn't easy to come by these days."

"And yet, here you are, out alone in the forest with me. I could be taking you anywhere."

I brushed a branch away from my face as I trudged onward. "Please. You have a gun and I don't, so I'm pretty sure if you wanted to kill me, you would have already."

Alec stopped in his tracks and walked back to me. He brushed my sweaty hair from my eye. "I would never hurt the girl who saved my life. That's a fact. Now come on, we're almost there."

"Back when the Consulate first rescued me, Dr. Sorokin said something about Callie City probably being on one of the outlying moons or planets. So are there other habitable places besides Caelia?"

Alec shrugged. "As far as the guns go, James told the Consulate that Callie City was on another planet. He figured it would discourage Consulate sweeps on Caelia if they thought the guns were elsewhere. What better place to hide than where they'd least expect to look?" The trees thinned out and a pinkish tinge crept across the sky. "And yes, there are some survivors who didn't want anything to do with the Consulate or the Resistance, and they struck out on their own within this solar system. A few of the outlying moons and planets are habitable, but barely. Nothing even close to Caelia. Nothing like what you're about to see." He scratched his head. "I don't get why you'd come all this way and choose one of those desertlike rock planets over this paradise, but to each his own."

The sun peeked out over the horizon. The two moons were faint but still visible. Maybe we were almost at Callie City. I couldn't wait to get there. I'd find James, locate the guns, destroy them for good, then figure out a plan to save my dad. What could possibly go wrong? A fresh burst of energy propelled me onward. That same delicious aroma I'd smelled outside the cave caught me again. Something about it reminded me of the weeks upon weeks I'd spent in a haze in the containment room.

"What is that scent?" I asked.

Alec pointed to my right. They were just visible in the breaking light. My heart almost stopped in my chest. A small tree held hundreds of pink flowers in full bloom. I walked over and touched the soft, velvety petals. They smelled like heaven, and I buried my nose in one and inhaled deeply. I wished Callie had been able to see this; she would have loved it.

"*Muy bonita*," Alec said. He appeared at my side and plucked one of the larger flowers. Then he reached up, tucked my hair behind my ear, and pinned the flower to hold it in place. "You deserve something beautiful. Do you really not remember anything from the containment center these last few months? Nothing from the time you got here on the Consulate ship to the time you found your dad?"

"Not really," I said. "A few times I thought I smelled flowers, and I still remember bits of that propaganda crap that they played through the sound system . . . and some strange dreams. But that's it. Why?" I wasn't about to mention that those strange dreams involved James kissing me.

Alec stared at me a minute and I worried that he was the one who was going to kiss me, but his mouth curled up into a smile. "No reason. Come on, you haven't seen anything yet." Then he took off running and I lost sight of him.

"Wait!" I yelled. I followed as fast as my sorry-ass legs would take me. I caught a glimpse of him up ahead and tried to go faster. Finally, I broke through the trees and Alec stood there waiting, a knowing smile on his face.

I gasped at what lay before me. It looked like the Infinity program, only better. Pink sand stretching out in all directions. Beyond that, aquamarine water as far as the eye could see.

The ocean.

Chapter FOUR

I TOOK OFF MY SHOES, PUT THEM IN MY SATCHEL, AND squished my toes into the pastel sand. It felt incredibly soft, like I'd stepped into a cloud. My eyes fixed on the sparkling, churning sea of blue.

Alec smiled. "Breathtaking, isn't it?"

I flashed him a smile and took off across the sand toward the water. My feet sank with each step until I reached firmer wet sand by the ocean's edge. A gentle breeze rippled across the water and through my hair. I hesitated and stared, hypnotized by the ever-changing waves undulating ahead. A wave broke and warm water splashed over my toes. I wanted to walk in a little farther but remembered the satchel at my side.

I turned to Alec, who was coming toward me. "It's amazing," I said. "I keep using that word but it's true."

Alec reached for my hand. "You're pretty amazing

yourself. I remind myself every day that I'm alive because of you."

I worried that he was confusing his feelings of gratitude for a whole different type of feeling. Not that I wasn't flattered. He was nice and cute enough. His dark, thick hair and muscled physique would make some girl really happy someday—I just wasn't that girl. If I'd had even a flicker of feelings for him that went beyond friendship, I would've gone with it. Life would be much easier without liking the boy who had tried to kill me. Unfortunately, I couldn't get that boy out of my head.

I gently extracted my hand. "Alec, I like you. It's just, just . . ."

"Just James, right?" He shrugged. "So I might have a chance too, if I shoot you?"

That wasn't fair. *But it was true.* "It's not like that. I—"

A ship came into view from over the trees. It was quiet, unlike the loud drone of other Consulate ships. I grabbed Alec's hand back and tugged. "Run!"

He shielded his eyes and looked upward. "No worries. It's one of ours."

The ship landed on the sand a short distance away. Alec grinned. "Come on. Let's get moving before the Consulate finds us."

We ran to the ship and boarded. It was similar to Markus' though a tad smaller. The pilot tipped his hat to me as I sat down. I pressed a button and a strap appeared around my waist to secure me in the seat.

Alec clapped the guy on his back. "Nice timing, *amigo*," he said as he sat next to the pilot. "Tora, this is one of our best pilots, Max. Max, meet Tora."

Max nodded in my direction. "I've heard all about you. Now let's get out of here."

We rose silently into the air. A million questions filled my head and started tumbling out. "Why didn't Markus come? He's a pilot. Where did you get a ship like this? How far away is Callie City? Are the guns there?"

Max turned to Alec, who frowned and shook his head slightly. What was that about? Max cleared his throat. "Markus hasn't been doing well. These days, he's usually too drunk to fly."

Alec met my eyes. "Ever since Britta died, he's been a mess. We can't pull him out of it."

I remembered the pain on Markus' face after she was killed, how he'd touched her cheek before they released her body into space.

Max cleared his throat. "As for the ship, it was created by one of our Resistance members. It's the only one like it for size and stealth. We need it in order to carry out our activities without Consulate interference."

I scanned the skies, hoping one of their ships wouldn't appear. Memories of them bombing the bunker until the door fell off weren't ones that I wanted to revisit.

"Callie City," Max continued, "is on the other side of the planet. As far from the Consulate headquarters as you can get without heading back into space."

Alec turned around to face me. "Caelia is a little bigger than Earth, so the Consulate realized they didn't have the manpower to patrol everywhere. They've claimed control of an area about equal to half the planet."

I frowned. "If the planet is bigger than Earth, wouldn't the days and nights be longer than on Earth?"

Max shook his head. "It's more about the moons than the planet size. The moon on Earth was closer and slowed the rotation of the planet. The moons here are farther away."

Good thing that Markus was part of the Resistance, otherwise I'd feel like the dumbest one around.

Max guided the ship higher until we were out of sight from the ground. I watched in awe as we moved through a wispy white intangible substance. These were actual clouds. So different from the empty red skies of Earth. It was exactly like the dream I'd had after James shot me when I saw Callie again. It had felt so real, but how could I have dreamed clouds when I'd never experienced them before now?

Thinking of Callie, I reached into the satchel and pulled out the picture she'd made. It had hung on our bunker wall and after she'd died, I'd faithfully straightened it every day, knowing how much effort she'd put into it. The pastel colors of the flower petals had faded a bit and one corner had bent from being jostled in my bag, but it was the most valuable thing I'd ever own.

Max's words pierced my reverie. "Those burners

assumed that everyone else had died. They didn't know the depth of the Resistance movement. Some were able to infiltrate the pod cities, blend in . . . even work at the Consulate."

Alec cut in quickly. "Others lived in bunkers outside of the cities, like your family."

I'd never even considered that there were other bunkers out here.

"Of course, they weren't as high-tech as your bunker," he added. "And they wouldn't have had an Infinity like you, which is why you thought you were alone on the planet, but our Resistance network was able to get the word out over the com systems once Caelia was found."

"So how many Resistance members are there?" I asked. "And didn't they check the Net for survivors?" I thought of all the messages I'd posted that had gone unanswered until Alec had come along.

"About fifty in Callie City," said Max. "We're the biggest settlement. There are a few other colonies on Caelia and on a nearby planet and moon, but I'd say no more than a hundred Resistance members total." He sighed. "And though I'd like to tell you that the Resistance was on the lookout for survivors, we were busy taking care of our own. We didn't even use the Net for fear that the Consulate would locate us. Just used secret com channels to communicate."

Alec agreed. "So they wouldn't have saved me either if it makes you feel any better. You were my only hope. Also, there are a few other colonies of people I told you about who aren't Consulate or Resistance. We're not sure of their exact numbers, but there can't be too many of them."

I sank back into the seat and tried to absorb everything Alec and Max had said. The Resistance movement was bigger than I'd realized. There had been other survivors with me on Earth, others who'd escaped the Consulate and had come to start a new life. I had no idea.

"But now there's all the water and air anyone could ever want," I said, confused. "So why is there still a Resistance?"

Alec shook his head. "Man may have traveled thousands of light-years from home, but what's that saying? 'Wherever you go, there you are.' They're still the same. We're all still the same."

Max looked back at me. "The Resistance doesn't care about water now. They care about revenge for all the innocent people murdered by the Consulate. All the ones who were killed for their W.A.R. machines or left to burn outside the pod cities."

Alec nodded. "The Consulate must pay for their crimes against humanity. They know we're out here somehow, and that your father's guns can be used against them at some point. They think the best defense is a good offense. They'll stop at nothing to wipe us out."

My father's guns would never be used against anyone if I could help it.

So many more questions popped into my head, but my eyelids felt heavier every second. The running, hiding, and drug withdrawal had wreaked havoc on my body.

"Rest, *ángel*," Alec said. "We have a few light breaks before we'll get to Callie City so you have time for a good nap. We're going to rest, ourselves."

Max flipped a switch that must have been the autopilot because he stretched his arms and leaned back in his seat.

I fought the exhaustion in my bones. A tiny voice told me what would make me forget about that exhaustion. The physical craving for the pain meds temporarily overwhelmed me. I shook my head. No way would I ever be that vulnerable again.

"What about Kale? Where's he? Where are the guns?" Back on Earth, Kale had been so focused on defeating the Consulate and growing the Resistance that he had no qualms about disposing of me when I showed no interest in his war. Especially when he realized James could fire my dad's weapons too, which I still didn't understand. Kale wanted to use the guns to destroy the Consulate, where I just wanted the weapons destroyed, period, so they couldn't hurt anyone again. I'd guess his goal of wiping out the Consulate hadn't changed since then.

Alec yawned. "Wish I knew the answers. After we outran the Consulate ship and that giant bomb you detonated, Kale made it to Caelia, dropped Markus and me off, and left again with a pilot named Gunther. Said he'd be back though." Alec patted Max on the shoulder. "After a few weeks in Callie City, Max brought me to the Consulate, and you know the rest."

I let my head fall against the seat and closed my eyes. Unanswered questions still swirled in my weary brain, but what mattered now was that we were on our way to Callie City. And when Kale did return, which I knew he would, I'd be waiting.

We flew over miles and miles of thick forest before we slowed and started to descend. I stared out the window in awe of this foreign planet that was so alive and thriving. Something caught my eye and I leaned closer to the side window. Every once in a while I'd catch a glimpse of something between the trees—clusters of small, brown, box-shaped things.

"What are those?" I asked, pointing out the window.

"Huts," said Max. "We live in small groups in the trees. Only about four or five huts each, that way the Consulate will have a harder time finding us all in a search."

I peered into the forest. "The huts almost blend in with the trees."

"Exactly. Natural camouflage," Max said as he landed the ship in a small clearing. "Welcome to Callie City."

Alec pulled his pack over his shoulder. "Thanks for getting us out of there, man."

Max tipped his head toward Alec. "Anytime. I gotta go . . . see you at the meeting. Stay safe." He turned and ran off into the woods.

I stared after him. "I've never seen so many trees before,

even on the Infinity programs. This is unbelievable."

The fresh, earthy scent of the trees filled the air. After the deep sleep I'd had on the ship, I hadn't felt so alive in years. My sister would have loved that such a beautiful place was named after her. We passed several of the clusters of makeshift huts I'd seen from the ship. "This is where people sleep," Alec explained. "During the day, they're usually in the middle of the city by the command center."

The huts were made of wood on three sides and a thermoplastic sheet hung on the front. I walked up and touched the thick, heavy sheet. I pulled it back and looked inside. Cots to sleep in just like in the containment center. Guess the small structures wouldn't support the weight of the hanging sleep chambers that had been in the bunker and on the ships.

Alec pointed to a circle in the middle of the huts. "That's the fire pit."

I frowned. On Earth, everything had been so dry and scorched that the idea of intentionally starting a fire didn't compute. "You make fire?"

"Yeah," Alec said. "I know. It's cool though, you'll see."

After another few miles, we reached a cluster of huts that lay along a small channel of running water. Alec followed my stare. "You might have seen something like that on the Net. It's a creek. You can swim in it, bathe in it, and drink it." He pulled a thermoplastic flask from his pack. "It's where they get the Caelia Pure. Or rather, one of the places. Freshwater creeks and rivers like this are all over the planet. The largest river is the one the Consulate built their city near."

"Let me guess. They named it Consulate River."

Alec laughed. "How did you know?"

"Just lucky." I watched the water tumbling over smooth rocks and wanted to dip my hand in it. I couldn't get over the fact that water was available everywhere. No way would I ever take this for granted.

"So this is us."

I turned my head back to Alec. "Huh?"

Alec coughed and gestured at the group of four huts. "This is my group. I thought you'd stay here with us. Don't worry. You'll have your own hut. Mine is next to yours. Technically, yours is Markus' but he never sleeps there."

I raised an eyebrow.

Alec sighed. "He's always either at the bar or passed out in . . . other huts."

I shook my head. He was back to his womanizing ways. "There's already a bar?"

Alec chuckled. "It was the first thing the Resistance built, after the command center of course."

He led me to a tree near the huts that had orange ball-shaped things on it. "This is fruit. You read about it on the Net, right?"

I nodded but found it hard to comprehend that I could eat something that grew outside. All I'd ever consumed was the gel from energy packets. Alec pulled one of the spherical orange objects from the tree and peeled off a skin of some kind. He handed it to me. "Here. It's not exactly like anything that grew on Earth according to the Net, but it's delicious. Might take your system a little bit of time to adjust to it, though."

I studied and sniffed the fruit. It had a tangy, pleasant smell. "How did you know it was safe?"

Alec grimaced. "We've had a lot of trial and error in the last few months. Luckily, severe vomiting has been the only downside to unsafe food so far. This type is safe, and a favorite of the Resistance. They distill it for alcohol when they're not eating it."

I bit into the fruit and juice spurted from it and dribbled down my chin. It was the most amazing thing I'd ever tasted. "You realize I can never touch energy gel again after this?" Without waiting for an answer, I sank my teeth into the round fruit again and devoured it in minutes. My stomach gurgled like it had no idea what was going on. I didn't care if I had adjustment issues with the fruit or not, no way was I stopping.

Alec's eyes sparkled. "I like a girl with an appetite. Anyway, they grow all over the place. There are some leaves here that are good too . . . and some animals."

My eyes widened. "Like dogs? You eat dogs?"

"No, no, never." Alec waved his hand emphatically. "These are big animals, again not like anything I saw on the Net, but they are really good. Trust me."

I crossed my arms. "I'll stick to these orange things,

thank you. I am not eating animals." My chin was sticky with juice. "I'm going to the creek."

"Suit yourself," Alec said.

I placed my satchel inside Markus' hut, then marched down to the creek and took a tentative step into the stream It was cooler than the ocean, and I reached down and splashed some on my face. I took another step and then another. Even standing in the center of the creek, it only reached to my knees. I sank down and sat, not caring about my clothes, and let the stream rush over me.

After a minute, I leaned back and let the water close over my head. Bubbles filled my ears and I realized that I couldn't breathe. I sat up, coughed, and gasped for air. Being underwater would take some getting used to. I tried again. After taking a deep breath, I lay back in the shallows then opened my eyes and stared up. The distorted images of trees and the sky swam in front of me. The grime, dust, and dirt of the last few years slid away. It was so quiet under the surface, only the gurgling around me. I'd never felt anything so peaceful yet so powerful.

I'd also never felt so energized. Whatever faced me ahead with James and Kale, I'd do it with clean hair. I stood up and shook the dripping water from my hair. I'd forgotten about the flower behind my ear until I saw it floating downstream out of reach.

I walked up toward the huts where Alec was arranging sticks in the fire pit. "That is the best thing I've ever felt in my life," I told him.

He had a mischievous look in his eye. "It's even better naked."

"I'll have to try that sometime . . . when I'm alone." Maybe he hadn't heard the part about me liking James. I walked over to a large rock by the huts and stood on it, my face tilted toward the sun where it peeked through the trees. The good thing about thermoplastic was that it dried quickly, though the shirt was a little stiff. The sunshine warmed me. I felt strong. I was ready.

I hopped off the rock. "Okay, let's do this. Take me to where I can get some answers."

"Cool. I really want to see Lucy, and we both know who you want to see." Alec grabbed another few pieces of fruit. "For the road."

I followed Alec through the trees to the next group of huts, maybe a quarter of a mile away. Alec peered into the first hut. It was set farther off from the other huts. *James and his space issues.*

"Anyone here?" Alec called out. "Lucy? James?" His voice echoed in the trees.

"Guess not," I said.

Alec scratched his head. "They must be at the command center. We can stop by the bar on the way. Doubt James will be there, but at least you'll be able to say hi to Markus, maybe talk some sense into him since no one else can. Oh, and here." Alec plucked another flower from a nearby bush and tucked it behind my ear. "You haven't seen James in awhile. Don't you want to make a good impression?"

The bar was little more than a dimly lit shack. A strange wood and metal structure sat atop its roof. Every few seconds the inner metal pieces rotated closer to a large groove in the wood. There were multiple grooves and each had a different marking on it.

I pointed. "What is that?"

"Our version of timekeeping," Alec said. "We had to create some sort of standard 'day,' since so few people have access to an Infinity. Each groove means six light breaks have passed—a new day. It would be hard to organize anything otherwise."

I stared at the intricate contraption another minute before entering the bar. Makeshift tables constructed from driftwood were scattered around the room in a haphazard pattern. People clustered around them on rough plank benches. It amazed me to see furniture made from something other than thermoplastic. The only thermoplastic items in the room were clothes and the drinking mugs. Someone must have brought a stash from Earth.

A long-haired man held some sort of wooden, stringed instrument that he played with his fingers. I vaguely recalled the instrument from the Net. His voice warbled earnestly as he sang something about fighting and freedom.

"I'm guessing he's not Consulate," I joked.

Alec laughed. "None of these *gringos* would be caught dead hanging out with the Consulate."

I raised an eyebrow at him. "You were Consulate and they hung out with you."

He shrugged. "Yeah, but I had to prove myself like you wouldn't believe to earn their trust."

I scanned the room. One group at a table clinked their mugs together and chugged the contents in apparent celebration. A group of girls at another table listened with rapt attention to the long-haired dude, swaying back and forth with the music. Then I saw Markus. Or, rather, the side of Markus as he made out with some girl against the wall. I pointed him out to Alec. "He doesn't look like he's coming up for air anytime soon, does he?"

"No. We'll stop by again on the way back from the command center. You want a drink or are you ready to go?"

The last thing I wanted to do was stick around and watch Markus stick his tongue down a girl's throat. "Let's get out of here."

As I turned, a movement caught my eye from the other side of the room. There was a small table I hadn't noticed in the far back corner of the bar. The light barely even reached the table. My breath caught in my chest. It was only his back, but I'd know him anywhere.

James.

And he wasn't alone.

Chapter FIVE

Reddish hair fell in waves over her shoulders as she leaned toward James, her mouth curved into a smile. His left arm rested on the table, and her fingers playfully walked up his muscled forearm as she spoke. I felt like I'd been punched in the gut and wanted to throw up. *So shooting you is okay but talking to another girl makes you sick?* I couldn't speak, so I grabbed Alec's arm before he could leave. He followed my gaze to the corner table.

"Oh, her," Alec said.

She looked up and noticed us staring. Her eyes fixed on mine and something flashed across her face before she removed her hand from James' arm.

My heart beat like crazy in my chest. I was so mad at myself for believing that even after everything he did to me, James still cared about me. *You shouldn't be mad at yourself; you should be mad at him. He shot you, remember?* Anger welled up and I grabbed a full mug from the nearest table, ignoring the protests of its owner. I stormed over to the table.

Alec yelled something that I couldn't hear because my ears throbbed with rage. James swiveled around, and the red-haired girl's eyes widened. It seemed to happen in slow motion. Just as his eyes met mine, my stomach dropped and I almost lost my nerve. *Don't let him fool you again.* I reached the table and threw the contents of the drink in his face.

"That's for trying to kill me. I'd do worse if I had a weapon." I turned to the girl. "Good luck, he's all yours. Oh, and be careful . . . he likes to shoot girls."

Alec stared at me slack-jawed as I stormed back over to him. "Now I'm ready to go," I said.

"Tora!"

Several people yelled my name at once. One of them was James. I'd know that gravelly voice anywhere. I turned toward the second person as I stomped out the door. It was Markus. Apparently the ruckus had been loud enough to pry him away from his make-out session.

Markus stumbled out the door after us with James close behind.

"Sweetcakes, it's so good to see you," Markus said loudly. "Come here and give me a hug." He bent over me and I almost retched from the fumes on his breath.

"You're drunk off your ass, Markus," I said, pushing his arms away. "It's good to see you, but not like this."

Markus swayed a bit on his feet and Alec helped to

steady him. "Easy there, *amigo.*"

James stepped in front of me. "Tora, I thought we've been through this already. What's wrong?"

What the hell was he talking about? We hadn't been through anything. I glared into those hazel eyes of his and refused to let them affect me. "What's wrong is that while I've been rotting away in a Consulate prison—after you tried to kill me, I might add—you've been making moves on the next girl. I don't know why I'm surprised."

He gave me a pleading look "You know that's not how it is. Just hear me out."

I put up my hand. "How would I know that? I'm done listening to lies. Just tell me where I can find Kale and the guns, and I'll be on my way."

Alec coughed. "And I'd like to know where my dog is."

Markus waved his arm in the air as his words slurred together. "That mangy mutt is jus' fine. She's tied to a tree behind the bar with a bowl of water. James takes her everywhere with him." He pointed a finger in my face. "In fact, that's the only bitch you need to be jealous of, heh heh." With that, he turned and vomited onto the nearest bush.

I couldn't believe this was the same Markus that had swaggered his way across the planet as a gunrunner. Now he could barely even walk. After he finished gagging, he stumbled over to a tree and passed out within seconds.

"He needs help before he drinks himself to death." I stared at his snoring form.

"I've tried," said James. "He won't let me."

Alec shifted back and forth. "Now that you're here, maybe you can talk some sense into him, Tora. I'm going to run and and get Lucy. Be right back."

"Fine, go." I waved him away. All I needed was information about the guns and I was out of here. I'd get Max to take me and the guns somewhere, and then figure out how to destroy them once and for all. The sky had turned a dusky shade of orange. The light break was ending quickly and I needed answers before it got dark again.

I crossed my arms and stared at James. "You were saying? Kale? Guns?"

He ran his fingers through his hair. "Kale knows you're alive. He'd have found out anyway, so I figured it was better if he heard it from me. That doesn't mean you'll be safe when he gets back."

"Not with you around, that's for sure," I said. "So if I'm in such danger, why was Alec supposed to bring me here—to a settlement that you renamed after my sister. What the hell is that about?"

James frowned. "Remember? The plan was for you to lay low until we got more intel. I didn't know you were going to show up yelling and causing a scene," James said. He looked around like he half-expected Kale to show up at any minute. I remembered how James had followed Kale's orders to the end, even when it meant killing me. All because of some bigger plan that Kale was involved in that James wanted to know about. My life had meant nothing compared to that.

My voice came out harsh and grating. "You think that was a scene? You have no idea what kind of scene I am capable of. I'll ask you one more time since you seem to have a problem with your hearing—where are the freakin' guns?"

He sighed. "No one knows. I swear. Kale moved them somewhere after he brought Markus and Alec here. Said something about going to try and get more Resistance recruits from the outer areas. Markus has been drunk ever since, and Alec's been . . . with you." James gritted his teeth.

Like I had a choice. Most of the past three months, I hadn't even known who was around me because I'd been a doped up, drooling mess. James' eyes drifted to my hair and then to Alec. "Nice flower. Where'd you get it?"

I reached up to touch my hair. I'd forgotten about the flower. I ignored his question. Let James think what he wanted. "And Kale?" I kept my voice hard and businesslike. But the longer he looked into my eyes, the weaker I felt.

James reached out to touch my hand. "Kale's only been back once. Word is that he'll be here again soon though."

I pulled away from him.

"Please, Tora."

The way he said "please" reminded me of a fleeting dream about him. I couldn't quite catch the memory and shook it off. James' lack of answers was getting on my last nerve. "So what do you know? Did you find out the 'something bigger' thing that Kale was part of—the thing that was worth shooting me over?"

James took a step toward me. "Yes, but I already told you all this. I never—"

Lucy tore around the corner, leash dragging in the dirt, and jumped on me. She licked my face like she hadn't seen me in years. I smiled despite my anger and patted her head. "Easy, girl. I missed you too." And it was true. The sight of those big eyes and wagging tail made me think she was the only creature worth trusting in the whole universe.

Alec rounded the corner. "Sorry, she took off and pulled the leash out of my hand."

"No worries. We're done here." I gestured at James. "Basically, he knows nothing about anything." I studied the darkening sky and the long shadows beginning to creep across the ground.

James pleaded with Alec. He sounded almost desperate. "Help me out here, man. Tell her. She doesn't remember. C'mon, I took care of your dog—you owe me."

Alec hesitated. "Thanks for helping with Lucy," he said, shuffling his feet in the dirt.

I whipped my head toward Alec. "Remember what?"

"Your first escape attempt," Alec said.

All I recalled was being told, while in a drug-induced stupor, that I'd run away once before. I stared blankly from James to Alec. "What about it?"

Alec spoke like the words were being forced out of him. "It was with him. You ran away with James."

Chapter **SIX**

No way. I'd run away with James but had no memory of the experience. Not that I remembered much of anything about the past few months. All I could recall were those few strange dreams in between med doses. I shivered. The air contained a noticeable chill now, and the sun had all but disappeared over the horizon.

James watched me and looked concerned. "Did Alec give you the med to help with withdrawal?"

Now Alec was the one on the defensive. "I couldn't find it. There wasn't time—"

James reached into his pack and pulled out a blue vial. The slender tube had a button on the bottom side and a rough surface on the top. He held it out toward me. "Look, this will stop any new symptoms."

Did he seriously think I was just going to put out my

arm and let him inject an unknown substance into me? Another chill grabbed hold of me.

"It's okay," Alec said. "That's the withdrawal med. I swear. It's the same thing I was going to give you back in the containment center."

James inched closer to me. "Please let me help you."

"Fine," I said. "Only because I believe Alec, not you." I held out my arm and glared at him. "So if I ran away with you, how are you here when I was still stuck in the containment center?"

James reached out and held my arm to administer the vial. Electricity shot through me at his touch. As he put the rough end against my forearm and pushed the button, I tried to focus on his words.

"I was being held there too. Alec snuck me into your room one night, and I asked you to run away with me. You said yes." James pulled the vial away but didn't step back. My chills had already vanished. His eyes pierced mine. "Honestly, first you slapped me and called me a burner for shooting you. But after I explained and asked you to come to Callie City with me, you agreed, but said that being with me would 'be only slightly more preferable than staying with the Consulate.' Is any of this ringing a bell?"

I shook my head. How could I have forgotten all that? Especially the part where he'd explained everything.

A look of amazement crossed his face. "Wow, they must have given you some heavy mem drugs after we ran. I heard they were experimenting with stronger versions."

He knew about the memory drugs. Guess that made sense. He was a medic and all. "But my memories from before the containment center came back. I just have no idea what happened when they were giving me the meds. Will I ever get those memories back?"

James had explained everything to me, and I couldn't recall a single word of it.

He searched my eyes. "I don't know. I don't agree with those kinds of drugs, so I've never used them. I hope you do remember though." He looked disappointed. "Anyway, Alec helped us escape the building, but right as we got outside the door another guard saw us. You begged me to go without you. You told me that you'd never be able to keep up and that we'd both be captured."

That sounded like something I'd say. Even when I was in top form, my running was pathetic compared to James'.

"Anyway," James said, "Alec promised me that he'd break you out and bring you here. He and I pretended to struggle so we wouldn't blow Alec's cover, and then I took off." James stepped closer and looked into my eyes. "Believe me, I never wanted to leave you. And I told Alec I'd be back for you if he couldn't get you out."

Alec reluctantly agreed. "Yeah, that's all true. After James got away, the Consulate started you on the really heavy mem drugs. Thought they could brainwash you to their way of thinking. I started to worry these last few weeks. You were way out there, *ángel*."

James clenched his jaw. If Alec calling me *ángel* made

James mad, I hoped Alec would call me nothing else. Since he had saved me, maybe I should start calling him *mi héroe*. James should love that.

"What about your girlfriend in there?" I asked sweetly. "She seems . . . friendly."

"She's not my girlfriend. Her name's Sonya and she's part of the Resistance." James stood close to me and the familiar knots started twisting in my stomach. "I told her all about you. She wants to meet you, but I told her to wait until we cleared things up."

"Good choice." I wanted to say that girls don't smile like that and walk their hands up the arms of boys for no reason, but I held my tongue. "I don't feel like meeting her right now—I'm sure she'll understand. It's dark and we need to go."

A loud snore echoed from the tree. "Besides, we need to get Markus back to the hut so he can sober up. He's no good to anyone like this." I challenged James with my eyes. "That is, if you can tear yourself away from your non-girl-friend."

His eyes met mine again. "Tora Reynolds, you and I are going to have a long talk again . . . and you'll remember it this time." My name on James' lips caused a shiver to run down my spine. He looked at Alec. "Let's get this guy back home. Tora can take Lucy."

Hearing her name, Lucy bounded up to me with her tail whacking around like crazy. I gripped her leash and ran my fingers through her soft fur. The sky had turned inky black. "How are we going to find our way?" I asked.

Alec smiled. "No worries, *ángel*. The stars will be out soon and will give us some light. Besides, I know the way."

James and Alec half-carried, half-dragged Markus through the forest while Lucy and I followed. Every once in a while, Markus grunted in his sleep. Lucy trotted by my side like she didn't have a care in the world. I couldn't even imagine what that felt like.

Sure enough, the sky soon shone with bright stars and the two enormous moons. We walked mostly in silence as we stepped around branches and tree roots. A small flock of birds took flight as we approached. They glowed a bright bluish color in the dark and cast off soft light as they flew, creating icy streaks across the sky. A strange howling erupted every so often. Lucy emitted a low growl in response and the fur on her back stood up.

"What is that?" I asked, though I wasn't sure I wanted to know the answer.

"An animal," James said. "They don't look like anything I've seen on the Net. They come out mainly after dark. Pretty big, aggressive things, but we should be safe if we stick together."

"One of the Resistance had to kill one in self-defense," Alec said. "Then someone got the idea to try and eat it. They're not bad if they're cooked."

I shuddered. Out of all the dangers I'd encountered, the thought of an attack by a hostile creature hadn't crossed my mind, much less eating it. I'd rather run into a Consulate guard given the choice between the two. Not that I'd heard a peep from a Consulate ship since we'd arrived here.

"The Consulate really hasn't found this place?" I asked.

"Not yet. They know the Resistance is around, though," Alec answered, panting between his words as he shifted Markus in his arms. "I overheard some stuff when I worked at the containment center. They're still establishing resources and manpower—I'd guess they're coming soon."

"And our plan is to be ready for them. Even though Kale complicates things," James added.

"You trust him?" I scoffed. "He's going to use the guns, with your help I assume, to defeat the Consulate. Which makes you guys the new Consulate, right?"

James sighed loudly. Why did he always sigh when I spoke? "Kale has connections that I need. I tried to tell you this before. It has to do with Autumn's . . . my whole family's . . . murders."

I froze. I remembered the photo I'd seen of a younger James with his little sister, Autumn. It was the only time I'd ever seen a real smile on his face. How he'd told me that Autumn had loved leaves the way that my sister loved wildflowers. How she'd died with her little hands wrapped around his legs under the fire of Consulate lasers.

"So you've been using Kale to get to them?" I asked.

"Basically," James said. "But it's turning out to be the worst idea I've ever had."

I was about to ask more when we reached the first encampment, the one with James' hut. He motioned at Alec. "Stop here a sec. I need to grab something." They placed Markus on the ground and he sat up, mumbled something incoherent, and lay down again.

James went into his hut and emerged a minute later. He strode up to me in the dark. "I want you to have something," he said.

He was giving me a gift? My heart thumped wildly in my chest. Stupid heart. He pulled my hand out and turned it palm up, then placed a gun in it. "Here, you should have one of these."

I studied the standard-issue weapon. "Seriously? Ithought you preferred to take these away, not give them to me."

There was that sigh again. "I had no choice. Believe it or not, I did it to save your life."

"And shooting me? Was that to save me too?" I lifted the shirt and tucked the gun into my waistband. Hopefully, my white shirt was too nondescript for him to notice that it was his.

He touched my hand again. "You're alive, aren't you? And you realize I'm the one that called the Consulate to send those ships? I told you all about it right before we planned our escape."

I refused to admit he had a point about me still being alive, though it was pretty obvious. "Can we just assume that I don't know anything that happened during that time? It's all one big blank. The last thing I remember before finding Dad is you shooting me . . . I assume you know about my dad being alive?"

James turned toward Alec. "What?"

"I had no idea," Alec said. "All I knew was that he was a 'high-profile' prisoner. Only Dr. Sorokin was allowed in his room until the day we found Tora in there. Then it all made sense."

"Whoa," James said. "That's incredible. How is he?"

"Not great," I said. Grief welled up in me at the thought of Dad still lying helpless in that place. "I'm hoping you all will help me get him out of there."

I couldn't see James' expression in the dark. He was quiet a minute. "We'll figure something out."

The stars twinkled above us and I studied James in the dim light. I wished he could tell me everything again right now, but we weren't alone.

Alec walked over to Markus and nudged him with his foot. Markus grunted and turned over. "Maybe he could stay here with you for the night?" Alec asked James. "It would save us from carrying his ass any farther. I can take care of Tora from here."

I saw the wheels spinning in James' head. "I'll get him on his feet. Best that I walk you all back to make sure you're safe." He headed down to the creek, which must have been the same one that ran by our encampment. James returned with a container full of water that he dumped over Markus' head.

He spluttered awake. "What the hell?" He wiped water from his face as he sat up and blinked, then looked around like he had no idea what was going on. I knew how he felt. Only my stupor had been involuntary.

Markus' eyes finally focused, landing on me. "Tora? Is that really you?" He got to his knees and pushed himself up from the ground.

"Yep, in the flesh." I walked over to Markus, and he gripped me in a bear hug like he hadn't seen me in ages. He reeked of alcohol. I patted him awkwardly, then stepped away.

"I've been worried as hell about you," he said.

More like he'd been worried about where he'd get his next drink. "I'm fine, Markus. It's you I'm concerned about."

Markus brushed dirt off of his clothes. "Nothing to be concerned about, sweetcakes. Just doing my thing."

I knew how much Britta had meant to him. I touched his arm. "Since when does 'your thing' mean drowning yourself in moonshine?"

He shrugged. "It's been hard for me. When I'm drunk, I forget about things for a while."

I remembered how good the Consulate drugs had made me feel. Like I'd be happy forever as long as I had them in my system. "I get it, Markus, I do. We'll help you through this, but you have to try."

James put up his hand. "Okay, we need to get you guys back to your huts."

We trudged through the woods. Alec and Markus went

first, followed by James, Lucy, and me. I was all too aware of how close I was to James, and distracted myself by focusing on Lucy.

"Is anyone else starving?" Markus asked after a while.

My own stomach grumbled in response. The fruit and energy gel were the only things I'd consumed in a long time. "Sorry, Markus, I don't have any gel packs on me."

"There aren't many of them left, anyway," Alec said. "Everyone eats local food now."

I didn't blame them. That fruit was delicious. "What besides the fruit?"

Another howl pierced the darkness. James moved closer to my side. "That."

Markus made a fire in a pit not far from our huts while I collected more kindling. I scoured the ground for the small, dry twigs that James told me were best for priming the fire. Lucy curled up near Alec's hut and watched us. Alec and James had disappeared, and had been gone for over an hour. On the plus side, the sky had started to lighten again.

"Do you think they're okay?" I asked Markus.

He prodded the fire with a larger stick. "Sure, they know what they're doing." The fire grew into good-sized flames. "Think there's anything to drink around here?" he asked.

"The creek is right behind you. Caelia Pure is the hardest thing you'll get while I'm around."

Markus grimaced. "You always were a hard-ass." He

dropped the stick by the fire. "Honestly, I'm not sure I can make it without a drink."

I walked over to the fire. "The Consulate had me drugged beyond belief. I made it through the worst withdrawal ever. If I can do it, you can too. James has something that will help."

He hunched down and warmed his hands by the fire. "Yeah, but you're stronger than me. Always have been."

I settled next to him. "I'm not sure about that. In any case, I'll help you through it. I need you strong."

He turned sideways to look at me. "You're not still thinking you can beat Kale?"

"I don't just want to beat Kale. I want to beat the Consulate too. And I want the guns back."

Markus laughed. "Suicidal much?"

"Not lately," I said. Not since I discovered I'd accidentally killed my little sister who I'd loved more than life itself. "If we find the guns and get rid of them, the Consulate and Kale will be powerless. Everyone will have regular ole guns and we'll have an even playing field. Then maybe everyone will leave each other in peace."

Markus tossed a twig into the flames. "I think you're forgetting those Consulate bombs. We don't have any of those. Plus, isn't it human nature to be burners? Don't you think people will always try to impose their will on others?"

The heat from the fire warmed my face. "Not all humans. But the ones who do sure cause more trouble than the ones who don't. I still have hope. Otherwise, all this"—I waved my arm at the new world around us—"is for nothing."

A grunting sound came from behind us. I reached for my gun and whirled toward the trees. Alec and James emerged, dragging something behind them. It was an animal—thankfully a dead one.

Alec grunted again as they brought the animal over to the fire. It was huge and had a large jaw that I guessed contained equally large teeth.

"Is that the same kind of thing that was howling earlier?" I asked.

"Yeah," said James. "Luckily, they are solo predators. They'd be hard to overcome in a pack."

I stared at the huge, dead-eyed creature. "It looks like it could bite me in half."

Alec patted the gun at his side. "Probably could, but they're no match for a laser between the eyes."

I saw blood oozing from Alec's hand. "It hurt you!"

Alec wiped the back of his hand on his shirt. "No, I cut myself on purpose. They're attracted to blood. It's fine—just a scratch, really."

James put a large stick over the top of the fire. It was propped up by several forked sticks that had been wedged into the ground around the fire.

"What's that for?" I asked.

Alec grinned. "Dinner. You might not want to watch the next part."

I went over to Lucy and stretched out next to her. She nuzzled her nose into my side, and I petted her while the men did whatever they were doing to the animal. Her doggy smell filled my nose as I drifted off to sleep.

I woke to the aroma of something I'd never experienced before. My mouth salivated and I wiped the drool with the bottom of my shirt.

"Come and get it, Tora," Markus called.

I stretched and strolled over to the fire pit. The thoroughly roasted animal had been severed into parts that were laid out on five trays. Alec brought one of the trays over to Lucy who ate her entire serving in what looked like one bite.

"Next thing you know, you'll be telling me we should eat dogs too. I am not eating an animal." I said, knowing as I spoke that I lied. My stomach gurgled in hunger, and I would have eaten a pile of dirt if it had been placed in front of me. The aroma of the meat was pulling at me, and I picked up the tray without thinking. "Fine, I might as well try it."

Alec returned with Lucy's empty tray and joined James and Markus around the fire. They dug in, tearing hunks of meat off the bone with their teeth. I watched for a minute, then sat by them and picked up a larger piece with my fingers. I sank my teeth into it. The outside flesh was crispy and the inside was juicy. It was strange having something with that much substance in my mouth. Even the fruit had been mostly liquid. I had to chew slowly, my teeth grinding the meat.

"Go easy," James warned. "This is your first time with solid food, and it will take your body some getting used to."

All I'd ever known until Caelia was energy gel. I'd read about food in my early years studying history on the Net but couldn't believe what I'd been missing. I swallowed another piece of meat. "This is surprisingly tasty."

They laughed. Markus tossed a large bone over the fire to Lucy who caught it in her mouth. "You want to try hunting yourself next time?"

I shuddered. I had no desire to face something like that on my own. Plus, the thought of killing it made me queasy. "I just want to eat it, not kill it."

Markus chuckled. "Hypocrite."

We ate in silence, stopping only to throw scraps to Lucy. I looked at the group around me, from Lucy to Markus, and felt something that was close to happiness.

"Have any of you swam in the ocean yet?" I asked.

Markus laughed. "Maybe, but I wouldn't exactly remember if I did."

James shook his head. "No, not much time for fun yet."

I wiped my mouth with the back of my arm. "I bet it's even better than swimming in the creek. My sister and I dreamed about it. As soon as I get the guns back and save Dad, I'm going swimming." My stomach had never felt so full before. A heavy sleepiness settled over me and I yawned. "But first, I need a nap."

"Hold up, what was that? Your dad's alive?" Markus

asked, eyes wide in the firelight. He'd been passed out when we'd talked about it earlier.

I nodded and stretched. "Yes, he's alive. I'll tell you all about it, but I'm so tired right now."

The stars twinkled against the dark sky, but I knew it would soon be light again. I curled up on the ground next to the warmth of the fire. The crackling sound of the flames lulled me into a trance.

"Good idea," I heard James say. "We should all rest a few minutes while we can. I'll stay out here with her."

Footsteps crunched in the dirt as Alec and Markus made their way to their huts. For a fleeting second, I realized I was alone with James. Unfortunately, my eyelids were too heavy to open and I drifted off into a dreamless sleep.

Chapter SEVEN

THE SUN SHONE WARM AGAINST MY SKIN. A SMALL STONE pressed into my cheek, and I blinked my eyes open to find daylight. I sat up and stretched to ease the stiffness in my back. The sleep pad from the bunker would have felt like heaven compared to this. My stomach rumbled in discomfort. Alec and James hadn't been kidding about my body not being used to this kind of food. I rubbed my belly, willing it to calm down.

The sound of muffled voices caught my attention. James crouched at the entrance to Alec's hut, but I couldn't make out what they were saying.

James nodded and stood, his pack slung over his shoulder. His build projected strength and confidence. It was hard not to stare. He startled when he turned my way. "I thought you'd sleep a while longer."

I combed a clump of dirt from my hair with my fingers. "All rested. Where are you going?"

He hesitated. "There's a meeting at the command center soon. I'm heading over."

"What's the meeting about?" I asked as I stood up.

James took a step closer and I tried not to notice the way the sunlight reflected off his blond stubble. "We've been planning how to address the problem of the Consulate once and for all. They haven't found us yet, but they will eventually. They know the weapons are around somewhere." He looked uncomfortable. "And I'm sort of in charge while Kale is gone."

It didn't help to shift my attention to his arms, which were as muscular as I remembered. Of course he was in charge—he was a natural leader. I really wished I could recall our escape together. I stood straighter. "I'm going with you." My stomach erupted in another loud rumble and I wanted to sink into the ground.

James shook his head. "No, it's too dangerous. Kale could show up. I need to figure out what he's planning first."

Kale's name sent shivers down my spine. Still, I didn't survive Earth just to hide. And now I had Dad to think about too. "What about rescuing my dad? What about that plan?" My voice rose despite my attempts to sound cool and collected.

Alec emerged from his hut, followed closely by Lucy, her tail wagging. She ran to James and licked his hand.

I whirled to face Alec. "You promised. You told me that we'd go back for him." I was almost shouting.

"*Sí*, I promised." Alec raised his hands. "And I've never broken a promise to you, have I, *ángel*?" He looked pointedly at James. "Max and some others will help us . . . they'll do anything to hurt the Consulate. We just need a good plan."

Markus stumbled out of the tent. "What's all the yelling about? Can't a guy get any sleep around here?" He rubbed his eyes. "I need a drink."

James took off his pack, reached inside, and pulled out another blue vial. "No, but you do need something to deal with the withdrawal."

"It works great," I said. I hadn't had a single symptom since James had given me the serum. "Why didn't you give Markus this med weeks ago?"

Markus cleared his throat. "I might have told James where he could put his vial once or twice." He looked embarrassed as he held out his arm. "Thanks."

"No problem," James said. "Still, I wouldn't recommend drinking again anytime soon. It won't mix well with the meds."

Markus groaned. "Where's the fun in that?" He grabbed his mug from where it rested near the fire and took a swig. I'm sure he wished it were anything but water.

I glared at Markus. I didn't have time for his pity party. "I don't care if you're having fun or not. Look, for some reason, my dad trusted you, Markus. You need to stay sober so you can make yourself useful. I need your help too. Got it?"

Markus looked at the ground and kicked the dirt, but nodded slowly.

James shifted his pack. "I've got to go to this meeting now or I'll be late."

"Me too." I ignored James' stare and patted the gun at my side. "I think I've proven that I can take care of myself."

Markus straightened. "I'm in. I'm going too." He had a strange gleam in his eye, like he wanted something. I knew that look.

"No," James and I said in unison.

"You know you'd never make it past the bar to get to the command center," I said.

James nodded. "You need to give the injection a little more time. It doesn't just prevent withdrawal symptoms— it stops the desire to ingest the substance that caused them. You'll be fine in another hour or so." He turned to Alec. "You should stay with Markus, keep an eye on him so he stays put."

Lucy sat at James' heels. By the way, you would think it was his dog and not Alec's. Alec looked as though he was going to protest. "I'll be right back after the meeting and then I expect both of you to be in a condition to help me."

Alec set his mouth in a hard line. "Take good care of her, *amigo*. The way I did when *I* got her here safely."

I put my hand on my hip and turned to James before he

could respond. "Guess it's you and me." I'd be alone with him in the woods. Maybe I should picture him shooting me every time my knees felt weak.

Our eyes locked. I tried to recall him aiming at me but what flashed through my mind instead was his fingers grazing my bandaged ribs under my shirt back at the bunker.

"Have it your way. Let's go," he said, marching away. I hurried to catch up.

Lucy followed us, which irritated Alec. "Lucy, come back," he called after us loudly. She turned and trotted back to Alec.

"She certainly seems to like you."

James moved quickly through the trees. "Yeah. Dumb dog, huh?"

I smirked. "You said it, not me."

We followed the creek back toward the command center. I was captivated by the gurgling water winding its way through the forest. The trees were lush, vibrant, and green—such a contrast to the brown, dead Earth I'd come from. Everything smelled fresh and alive, punctuated by the occasional aroma of flowers.

I got so caught up in my surroundings that I had to jog to catch up with James. I'd forgotten how fast he was.

"When was the last time you saw Kale?" I asked, breathing heavily.

James glanced at me over his shoulder. "A few weeks ago. Said he was going to find the leader of the Resistance and bring him back so we could finalize our attack on the Consulate."

I moved a wayward tree branch out of my way. "Who's the leader?"

"Don't know," James said. "And Kale doesn't know either—he said the guy preferred to lead from behind the scenes after some of his closest men were killed by the Consulate. They only spoke over the com system and the guy never said his real name." James paused and looked unsure whether to go on.

"What?" I asked.

"Kale did find out who killed my family."

My stomach dropped. That must be the info he'd been wanting from Kale all along. The info he'd risked my life to get.

My voice came out in a whisper. "Who?"

His eyes hardened. "Guy named Allan Davis."

I gulped, remembering the day Dad had brought me to work with him and we were called into his boss's office. How I had wiped my hand on my pants after enduring his sweaty handshake. "No way! I met him. He's the one who gave my dad the Infinity." The Infinity that Kale took from me.

James stopped and tracked back to me. "What? You know what he looks like?"

"Sure, but I was, like, nine years old." I told James what I recalled of the brief encounter, including how Davis had been in charge of the weapons department.

James shook his head. "He's in charge of most things, it seems. Kale told me that Davis was the one who hired him to come after you on Earth. He used a middleman to make the deal. No one in the Resistance knows what Davis looks like. Not even Kale."

Was it possible that I was the only one who knew what Davis looked like? Dad did, but he was a prisoner. Not for much longer, though.

"So what you're saying is that you need me, James." My heart began thumping faster at his nearness. *Don't go all girlie now.* I shrugged and tried to play it cool. "Maybe needing me means that even though you tried to kill me, you feel differently now."

James closed the last step between us. I stepped back, right into a tree. He grabbed my hands and pinned them to my side, his mouth inches from mine. "I didn't try to kill you," he growled into my ear. "I'm a perfect shot, remember?"

Before I could react, his lips closed over mine. For a minute I got lost in the sensation of his mouth on me. I kissed him back and enjoyed the ripples running through my body.

Then I remembered James standing in front of me pointing my own gun at me. I pushed off the tree and freed my hands from his. "If you think that was an adequate explanation about why you shot me, you've spent too much time in the sun. You can't go from wanting to kill someone to wanting to kiss them."

James stepped closer again but kept his hands to himself. "If we weren't already late, I'd show you exactly how I feel about you." He stared at me a second. "I promise I'll explain when we have more time. We can't miss this meeting."

"Right, the meeting," I said, ashamed that I'd kissed him while Dad was still imprisoned across the planet. I was a horrible daughter.

No, just a human one.

I ignored the voice in my head as I stomped behind James toward the command center.

We soon reached another shack-like building that was even smaller than the bar. Two men stood guard at the entrance. One of them tipped his hat to James as we approached. *"Hola, jefe."*

James gestured my way. "This is Tora. She's with me."

"Got it. Welcome, Tora." The same guy opened a thin, crooked door and waved us through. It's good they had guns to help them guard the place because I probably could have taken down the door myself.

Inside, a man at the front of the room spoke in Spanish to a group of forty-some people seated on wooden plank benches. He paused when we entered, nodded to acknowledge James, then continued. The heads that had swiveled toward us turned back to the speaker. James and I slipped onto a bench in the back.

"Why is he talking in Spanish?" I whispered. Though I knew some basic words from when my sister and I played around on the Infinity, I had no clue what this guy was saying.

James leaned over. "That's Edgar. He's in charge of basic operations. This is an update-and-planning session. All plans are made in Spanish. Since the Consulate banned all languages except English, no one there can understand what we're saying. We use the Net for the Spanish lessons. You might want to check into that." He smiled. "Don't worry. I'll explain what he's saying later."

His breath in my ear made my stomach do flips. *Act calm.* "Sure, that'd be great. But doesn't Alec speak Spanish? He was Consulate? They can't be that dumb."

"They're not dumb, they're arrogant," James whispered back. "The Consulate thinks they can control everything around them. They believe that if they declare English the only acceptable language, no one would dare think otherwise. Alec told me one guy was overheard saying *hola* back on Earth and was shot on sight."

"So Alec hid his Spanish from them?"

"Yes." James nodded. "But he wasn't typical Consulate. When I was in the containment center, Alec told me that the Consulate believes the new city is exactly what they envisioned. Everyone believes what they want them to believe and speaks how they want them to speak."

I stared ahead and tried to latch on to the few words I knew. *Muerto. Sangre. Consulate* was the same in both languages. Edgar's intense speech was a far cry from my sister and me discussing our pretend swimsuits on a virtual beach in broken Spanish. If only Edgar would count to ten or name some colors, I'd be golden.

Most of the others in the room were about my age, and most were boys. I glimpsed the red hair of the girl from the bar a few rows ahead. She turned to glance back at James a few times, totally ignoring me. Anger welled up when I thought about her walking her fingers up James' arm.

Edgar continued for a few more minutes and then he called out to James in English. "Anything to report?"

James stood. I understood the words, *Alec*, *Consulate*, and *pistolas*, and guessed he was telling the group what Alec had overheard in the containment center about the Consulate preparing a widespread search for Resistance troops and the bioweapons.

Sonya turned to face him when he finished and spoke in crystal clear English. "Then where is Kale with those weapons? Has he been in touch through the com? We need him."

I bit my tongue. Those were *my* weapons. And I needed Kale about as much as I needed a sun storm.

James stared at her calmly. "Kale should be back soon. We'll be fine."

She eyed him a moment longer, then flung her hair over her shoulder. "If you say so."

He gestured for me to stand. "One more thing," he said to the group. "This is Tora Reynolds, the girl I told you about who was being held in the containment center."

Several *holas* and hellos echoed around the room. I hated being the focus of everyone's stares and gave a quick wave before sitting down again. James told them about my dad and how he was recently discovered to be a Consulate prisoner. His relaxed posture belied the confidence and strength in his voice. "Long story short, we're going to get her dad back. When we meet again, I'll be asking for volunteers and we'll discuss a rescue plan."

I stared at James, openmouthed. I had hoped he'd help with my dad, but I hadn't realized how much power he held in this group or that he would use his influence to help me. James flashed me a quick smile when he sat. I wouldn't forget that he'd shot me, but he'd just earned a little more of my trust.

A few other people in the room stood and gave brief updates, also in English. I found these reports interesting. They included plants, nuts, and fruits that had been discovered since the prior meeting. Three people had vomited, and one almost died, after eating the same berry, so the Resistance was compiling a list of unsafe foods that would be posted on the Net. James told me that they'd been able to secure several Infinities from Consulate spies and kept one in the command center for common use.

When the meeting ended, the red-haired tramp immediately marched back to us. I found the sharpness of her nails disturbing and the defiance in her face unmistakable. Her eyes bored into mine. "I don't believe we've been properly introduced." She cast an accusing glare at James before settling her focus on me again. "I'm Sonya." She extended her long nails toward me.

I wanted nothing to do with her, but didn't want to look weak. "I'm Tora," I said as I took her hand.

Her nails dug into my wrist. "I know exactly who you are." She smiled sweetly, which contradicted the death grip she had on my hand. "You killed my brother."

Chapter EIGHT

I WRENCHED MY HAND FROM HERS. "EXCUSE ME? I DON'T know what the hell you're talking about."

"Sonya, you know that's not how it happened," James said. "It was a sun storm."

Sonya crossed her arms. "A sun storm wouldn't have thrown my brother into a cactus in the first place if it wasn't for her."

I remembered the guilty relief I'd felt when the soldier flew through the air and was impaled on a massive cactus spike. It had taken down one of the five people who had been shooting at me. "Not to nitpick, but your brother was trying to kill me at the time."

Sonya's eyes were cold and calculating. She didn't respond.

James sprang in between us. "Sonya, let it go."

She narrowed her eyes at him. "So, this is how it is,

James?" Her eyes were filled with hatred when they turned back my way.

I had flashbacks of when Britta stuck me inside a transport container. At least I'd liked her in the end. I had a sneaking suspicion that Sonya would never grow on me.

"Tora's on our side," James said. "And, like I've told you before, we're together. Got it?"

Her eyes flashed with anger, then softened. "Got it," she mumbled.

Edgar stepped up to us. "Everything okay here?"

James nodded. "Yes. Tora, this is Edgar. Edgar, Tora."

Edgar's intimidating build was offset by his kind eyes. "Nice to meet you," I said, trying to ignore the steady gaze of Sonya who hadn't moved.

Edgar smiled. "You too. The little I've heard about you from James has been glowing."

Yeah, James would never be accused of being verbose but I was still surprised he had talked about me at all. Getting him to string more than a few sentences together constituted a miracle.

"Hey there, remember me?"

The pilot who'd rescued Alec and me from the beach joined us, standing near Edgar. "Sure, good to see you again, Max." At least some faces were friendly.

A girl with straight blond hair stepped forward timidly. "I've heard so much about you," she said. "It's great to meet you. I'm Reed."

Sonya snorted.

"Hi, Reed." When I shook her hand, she leaned in and whispered in my ear, "Don't worry about Sonya."

I smiled and resisted the urge to tell her that Sonya was the one who should be worried. "So when do we meet again? Do we need to do anything?"

James cleared his throat. "You just need to stay safe and keep your ears open. We'll meet back here same time tomorrow."

Edgar nodded. "I think we're almost ready, sir . . . with or without Kale, no disrespect. It sounds like a Consulate search is coming sooner rather than later."

I'd prefer never having to set eyes on Kale again, but I still had to find my father's guns. I wasn't sure exactly how to destroy them yet, but I'd think of something.

James studied Edgar. "We'll give Kale another few days; still you're right that we need a backup plan. Let me think and we'll discuss it at the next meeting." He turned to me. "We should get going."

The group dispersed and James turned to Sonya. "Are you on board, or what?"

She twirled her hair. "Of course, you're the leader. I'm just one of your minions. That's all I'll ever be, right?" Pain flashed through her eyes before the defiance returned and she stormed out the door.

"She's pleasant," I said. "Might want to vet your minions a little more carefully in the future."

James touched my arm and a shiver ran through me. "Don't worry about her. She and her brother were really close. She's just looking for someone to blame."

We headed out the door, and I was still awestruck by the beauty of the vibrant flowers and trees. I hoped we could take care of the Consulate and Kale once and for all, because I never wanted to leave this place.

"Are we headed back to Markus and Alec?" I asked.

James shook his head. "Not yet. I need to talk to a few of the men stationed at the bar first. It'll only take a few minutes."

What I wanted to say was that he needed to talk to me and explain some things. Instead, I said, "Sure, no problem."

He told me that some soldiers were always on guard outside to watch for Consulate ships. So far, none had been spotted on this side of the planet, but if Alec was right, that would change very soon. We reached the bar and he squeezed my arm. "Be right back."

He walked over to two men standing near the side of the bar. They bent their heads in conversation with James, and I studied the sinking light in the sky. I'd spent so many years underground in the bunker that I'd barely known the difference between light and dark then anyway, aside from the screeching of the night storms.

"Tora! Come here." Reed was leaning out of a small makeshift window.

James was still in deep conversation with the men, so I ducked into the bar's entrance. Reed was sitting with some of the people I'd seen at the meeting. She patted the bench next to her. The others nodded at me and smiled as I sat down.

I smiled back. "I only have a few minutes."

Reed pushed a mug my way. "Here, have some water. Isn't that cool to say? 'Have some water.' I can't even believe I'm living on a planet where there's water to drink everywhere. We've been here a few months now, but it still feels like heaven."

I took a long sip from the mug. She was right. Chronic thirst had been a staple in my life. A place where I could drink water anytime I wanted sounded like heaven to me too. "Thanks."

It appeared that most of the meeting attendees had stopped in here afterward. Luckily, Sonya wasn't anywhere in sight. It seemed like the majority of the people weren't drinking water . . . I hoped Markus stayed away from this place in the future. He'd be useless if he fell back into his obliterated ways.

"Look," Reed said, "we just wanted you to know that we're really glad you're here. James told us all about you."

I raised an eyebrow. "I'm not sure I want to hear what he said."

A boy farther down the table laughed. "It was all good, I promise. Mostly about how kick-ass you are. I mean, taking down a Consulate ship on your own is awesome."

"Yeah, tell us about taking down that ship," another girl said.

I squirmed in my seat. James might think I was tough,

but I felt anything but when he was around. "That's nice of him," I said, "but I really only shot the wing and the ship crashed. Not a big deal."

Reed shook her head. "That's totally a big deal. I want to be more like you—tougher, I mean."

I studied her. "So how did you end up with the Resistance?"

Reed shrugged. "Same as most people here, I guess. Dead family, little hope, and then I got lucky when I ran into fellow survivors who shared their water and air. They turned out to be Resistance members, and I was all for joining a group that would destroy the Consulate." She looked around like she was worried someone might overhear. "But I prefer to be more of a helper, errand runner. I can't stand violence and hope I never have to use my gun."

I smiled. "We're not that different. I've just had to use mine, is all." If Reed really was an errand girl, maybe she'd have some good info. "What do you know about Sonya? Aside from the fact that she hates me?"

Reed scooted closer. "Personally, I don't think her issues are totally about her brother. I mean, they were close and all, but being a soldier means you could die. They both knew that." She lowered her voice even more. I had to strain to hear her. "I think it's more because of James."

My stomach lurched, and not from the meat. I'd been right. The way Sonya had smiled at him and touched his arm earlier had said it all.

"She met James back when he and her brother, Saul,

were recruited to the Resistance by Kale. She was always going on about how smart James was. Cute too."

I swallowed. I knew exactly how smart and cute he was. And deadly.

"Anyway," Reed said. "I think she had hoped that something would happen between them when he returned. After James escaped from the containment center, he showed up out of the blue one day. I've never seen Sonya light up the way she did when he walked into the command center that first time."

Reed took a sip of her water. "James doesn't say much, but everything he did say in those first days was about you. I could tell that it pissed her off royally. But when you didn't show and you didn't show, I think she thought you might never get out. She started flirting with him again. Told him to wait a little longer when he started talking about going back for you."

"Thanks for telling me," I said. "It explains a lot." You'd think I would be used to people wanting me dead by now.

We drank our water and reminisced about our lives on Earth.

"I never thought I'd live to see a place like this," said a husky boy named Web. He looked like he could lift the entire table up with one finger if he wanted to. "Seemed like the last view I'd have was of that giant blazing ball of hell. When Trent and Ian hit me up through the com and told me about Caelia, I'll admit that I cried like a baby."

Reed patted Web on the shoulder. "I think we all did."

When the table fell silent, I took a chance with the group. "What do you know about Kale and this Resistance leader he's looking for?"

Web scoffed. "Between you and me, I think Kale's an asshole. James never said why Kale wanted to kill you, but I can't say that I'm surprised."

"Yeah," another guy added. "Honestly, I think the whole search thing is a cover-up." He leaned into the table. "Think about it. This supposed Resistance leader is the perfect scapegoat. Whenever Kale tells us something we don't want to here, he just says it's 'orders' from his leader. Kale supposedly didn't even know where this person was when he went off to find him. Weird, no?"

He had a point. I raised my eyebrow. "Then where do you think Kale is if he's not searching for the leader?"

The boy shrugged and Web answered. "Beats me. Maybe it has something to do with all those guns of yours he took. That sucks by the way. James told us all about it."

My stomach sank. No one seemed to know Kale's whereabouts. "But Kale was also rounding up other recruits. He must have some people loyal to him here in his camp."

Reed nodded. "Some agree with Kale that all possible force should be used against the Consulate. Others agree with us that the weapons will only end up bringing more destruction. We *all* agree that we need to do something. We just can't agree on what."

I'd all but forgotten that I was supposed to be waiting for James when he came bursting through the door of the bar.

I stood up. "I'm right here. Sorry, I was just talking—"

"Hide," he said. "Kale's here."

Chapter NINE

I BROKE OUT IN A COLD SWEAT. MY MEMORIES OF KALE involved him trying to hurt me. That, and taking away my Infinity, which still ticked me off. I crouched down and Reed motioned for me to crawl behind the bar that was near our table. The guy tending bar waved me to the corner by his feet while he kept pouring moonshine.

I'd barely tucked myself underneath when the door crashed open again and I heard Kale's booming voice. "Long time no see, my young soldiers. How the hell is everyone?"

A few men cheered boisterously. Aside from that, only a smattering of applause filled the room. Heavy steps approached the bar. I held my breath and pulled my legs up to my chin.

"How's it going, sir? Get you a drink?" the bartender asked.

"Abso-fuckin-lutely," Kale responded. He sounded like when he was on the pain meds back on Earth.

Kale guzzled the liquor. Seconds later, the glass slammed back down on the counter. "Damn, that's good. I'll take another. Been forever since I've had a good drink."

Other footsteps came over. "Sir, what's the news?" James asked.

The glass clinked on the counter again. "Give a guy a minute to relax," Kale said. "One more," he added as more moonshine splashed into his glass.

After the glass clinked down on the counter for the third time, he addressed everyone in a loud voice. "Let me fill you in. One, I've got people in other colonies willing to help us. Some of them set up shop on the planet Dais, and let me tell you, that's one hellhole of a place. We need to fight for Caelia by taking down the Consulate once and for all."

A few drunken cheers erupted from the other side of the bar.

My thighs burned and I didn't know how long I could hold myself up. I tried to shift my legs and knocked my knee into the side of the bar. The bartender dropped a cup on the counter, and I knew he was trying to cover for me. "Here, have another drink," he said to Kale.

"Don't mind if I do." I heard the sound of the liquid as he gulped it. "You know, I used to think we just needed to stop the Consulate and we'd be fine. I realize now that we need to be the ones in power—create our own government—to stop burners like that from ever being in charge of anything again."

Good thing he wasn't on a power trip or anything.

"So what's the plan?" James asked.

Kale smacked his lips. "Good news and bad news, James. The good is that I found the leader of the Resistance. "

Shocked gasps and whispers filled the room. Apparently more than a few people had bought into the theory that Kale had made this leader up.

"So, what's the bad news?" James asked.

"He needs a medic. I need you to come with me. And you won't believe who it is."

"Okay," James said quickly. "Show me the way."

Kale stormed back across the bar and yelled to no one in particular on the way out the door: "The time has come, soldiers. As soon as our leader is back in shape, we're taking down those Consulate bastards!"

With that, the door slammed shut. James leaned over the bar, whispering to me, "Get back to the huts and stay out of sight. I'll come find you as soon as I can."

Just like that, he was gone. I exhaled slowly and extended my legs. They'd started to cramp. The bartender helped me to my feet.

Reed was standing, looking out the window. She turned to me. "It's all clear. They went the other way. Go before it's full dark."

She didn't need to tell me twice. I stepped out of the bar

into the twilight. The only people in sight were the guards James had been speaking with earlier. They motioned me toward the woods, which was where I was planning to go anyway. Before I'd even run ten feet, huge drops of water splashed on my head. I froze in place and stared up. *What the hell was this?* Despite the darkening sky, I could easily make out huge swirling clouds. They looked like the white ones we'd flown through earlier, except black and angry. Wind whipped my hair around my face.

"What's going on?" I whispered to the men.

"A big-ass storm from the looks of it," one said. "The rain will only get worse."

Rain. I remembered the word from the Net but had never been able to imagine water just falling out of the sky like that. This was crazy.

"Better run faster," the man said.

Run faster. Ha. They didn't know they were already witnessing my max speed. I took off again and made it into the trees just as a huge flash of light filled the sky. It was followed by a deafening clap and I covered my ears. The rain pelted down and bit into my skin. I shivered as the cold water drenched my clothes, and my shirt began to stiffen. They were going to have to figure out some new clothing now that we didn't need thermoplastic anymore because being wet in plastic sucked. The trees overhead did little to protect me, since it seemed as though the rain was coming at me sideways. The tops of the trees bent in the ferocious wind. I fought my way forward with every step. At least the night storms on Earth hadn't involved ice-cold rain.

On top of everything else, if it wasn't full dark yet, it was pretty damn close. I shielded my eyes from the onslaught of rain and tried to locate the creek. Between the wind, blackness, and torrential downpour, I couldn't see more than a foot in front of me. I started to panic and ran in what I thought was the direction of the huts. My feet slipped and caught on a tree root. I crashed to the ground, my ankle twisting as I fell.

I pushed myself up and took a tentative step. Sharp pains shot through my ankle, and I hoped it was a sprain and not broken. I limped along for several minutes but got turned around again, so I stopped to try and get my bearings. For all I knew, I was going in the wrong direction.

The lashing of the wind and rain had intensified and I couldn't see anything aside from the occasional jagged flash of light. I shivered, beyond freezing in my clothes. I had no idea how long this would last but it already seemed longer than the sun storms on Earth. I felt my way to the nearest tree and crouched down, huddling against the base, trying in vain to shelter myself from the elements. My ankle throbbed.

After awhile, my thighs burned and I couldn't crouch a minute longer. I lowered myself to the ground, which was so soaked with water that my butt sank right into it. *Perfect.* Between hiding under the bar and taking refuge under a tree, I'd been in that position enough for a lifetime.

Crouching and catheter removal were things I'd love to not repeat anytime soon.

About an hour later, the rain finally let up and the wind died down. I stood and stretched my legs out, while my ankle screamed in protest. Without the wind and clashing sounds in the sky, the night was quiet—too quiet—like someone had turned off the planet's sound. I started walking, even though I had no idea which way to go. There was a hint of dull gray so it couldn't be too long before another light break. The good news was that the clouds were starting to break up, and I caught occasional glimpses of the two moons. I could finally see a little bit around me, despite the light rain still falling. The bad news was that the creek was nowhere in sight.

Worse, my gun was soaked. When I tried to test it out, it wouldn't fire. Since there was no water on Earth, the manufacturers hadn't had to worry about designing water-proof weapons. Guns only had to be heatproof.

I sighed in frustration. Had Dad thought about that potential issue when he designed the super-weapons, or had he also been focused solely on Earth's environment? What was I supposed to do now? Since I'd only ever lived in a pod city or bunker, I knew squat about surviving in the natural world. The two moons peeked through another break in the clouds, along with a smattering of stars, and created more light. Shame I didn't understand the strange Caelia sky well enough to know how to follow them.

Wait. Alec had pointed out a constellation when we were standing outside the cave. Something about the crying boy and the stars being his teardrops. I found an open space between two trees, then squinted hard at the sky. Yes, there were the boy's eyes with the trail of stars under them. It was as good as any direction to try, so I headed toward the Weeping Boy. Something near me moved in the darkness and I froze.

"Hello?" I whispered as my voice cracked. *Please don't be the Consulate. Please don't be Kale.*

There was total silence for a long moment before I got my answer. A long, shrill howl pierced the air. It was almost identical to the one that had belonged to the ferocious-looking animal we'd eaten earlier.

How ironic that now I'd be the one eaten.

Chapter TEN

As it grew even closer, the howl morphed into a snarl. I was so done for. My ankle felt like it had swelled to twice its normal size. Though I'd never be able to outrun the creature even in my best condition, I certainly couldn't out-hobble it. I grabbed for my gun but it was still waterlogged and wouldn't fire, so I reached down in a desperate attempt to find anything I could use to defend myself. My fingers curled around a broken tree branch that was just visible in the dark gray light, and I lifted it into the air.

I wanted to laugh and cry at the same time when I realized it was only about six inches long and the width of my pinkie finger. Just when things couldn't get any worse, the creature charged. I registered its massive size and glowing red eyes before it lunged. I ducked and rolled on the mud-soaked ground, snapping my pathetic twig in the process. *Awesome.*

Something trickled down my face and I tasted blood in my mouth. I reached up and felt the jagged claw marks on my cheek. My face stung sharply as the light rain made contact with them.

The huge beast circled around to face me, teeth bared. *That is a whole lot of teeth. I'll be shredded in one bite.* I scanned the ground again and saw nothing but equally sad twigs and one smallish rock.

The rock was slippery from the rain, but I grabbed hold and hurled it at the animal with as much force as I could muster. The beast was hit right in the face. It winced and shook its head back and forth before sizing me up again. Not quite the rapid retreat I'd been hoping for.

I pulled the gun out a second time but wasn't surprised when nothing happened. It would be a miracle if the gun ever worked again. I looked around in a panic. The ground was rockless, the gun was useless, and I was about to die.

The creature snarled again but hesitated. Maybe the rock had thrown it off-kilter. I watched the animal and grew angrier. No way had I survived Earth and made it to another planet only to die like this. *Screw that.* I grabbed several more puny twigs and raised one over my head, then yelled at the top of my lungs. I didn't care who heard me. I shouted and threw twigs as I moved toward the animal.

I'm not sure how threatening I looked—probably more crazy than scary. In any case, it snarled but backed up as I came toward it. My voice grew hoarse—my war cry would soon sound like a war whimper—so I jumped in the air and threw the last stick with one last strong holler. When I landed on my hurt ankle, the holler turned into a raspy shriek.

The creature turned and ran off into the trees. I doubt I'd really scared it, but it must have thought I wasn't worth the effort. Most of its prey was probably easier to catch and much less obnoxious.

I limped on for a while and wanted to shout for joy when I spotted the creek. The Weeping Boy had saved me. I glanced at the lightening sky in gratitude. Pink rays of sunshine sliced through the clouds. A slight drizzle started and stopped as I trudged through the wet ground, my shoes making sucking sounds in the mud. My ankle hurt, my cheek stung, and I was filthy, but I was alive.

I spotted our group of huts as the last clouds disappeared and streaks of golden sunlight filled the sky. Markus sat with his back to me and watched Alec throw a stick to Lucy. She bounded toward the twig, then turned and raced full throttle toward me. It reminded me of the first time I met her in the Consulate building where all the other animals had starved. She'd run toward me like she somehow knew I was a good guy. I patted her head and she trotted by my side.

"Tora!" Alec called when he saw me. "I'm glad you're okay, that was some *loco* storm, huh?" His eyes widened in alarm as I got closer. "What happened to your face, *ángel?*"

"Just got into a little scuffle with one of those tooth monsters. Why, how bad does it look?"

Markus stood up and walked over. "It looks pretty impressive, if you ask me."

Alec gaped. "I can't believe you took on one of those *criaturas* by yourself."

"Like I had a choice."

"That's my girl," said Markus.

Alec's brow furrowed. "Those cuts need to be treated or they could become infected. You need a medic." His expression darkened. "Speaking of which, where is James? Wasn't he supposed to be taking care of you?"

I straightened my shoulders. "I don't need anyone to take care of me. Anyway, he was needed to tend to someone else. Kale's back."

Markus looked pale. "Shit. Did he see you?"

I shook my head. "No, but his return is a good thing. Now you can both help me find out where he hid my guns."

Markus sighed. "Looks like I picked the wrong week to quit drinking."

I punched him in the arm. "I'm serious, Markus. After all that crap you put me through over those guns, you're going to help me."

He snapped his hand to his head in a mock salute. "Yes, ma'am."

Alec stared at us like we were crazy. "This is serious. Kale won't love seeing you around, Tora. You should try to stay out of his way for now."

I smiled. "That's why you boys will have to be my eyes and ears. We have to stop Kale and destroy the guns." I tapped my finger against my chin. "And we need to come up with a plan to save my dad."

Markus chuckled. "Good thing you're not an over-achiever."

"Ha, ha. Now I need to think. I'm going down to the creek. Let me know when James gets back."

As I limped down to the stream, I overheard Markus say to Alec, "I love a woman who takes charge."

I sat on the edge of the creek and dipped my feet into it. The cool water felt surprisingly good on my injured ankle. My head spun as I tried to think through everything. We had to somehow rescue my dad from the Consulate and stop Kale from whatever craziness he was planning. Dad was still on the other side of the planet, Kale was here, and the guns could be anywhere.

As much as I hated those weapons, I didn't see how I could save Dad without using them. It bothered me that I kept finding excuses to use them, just like when I'd shot down the Consulate ship. But the Consulate were the bad guys, not me.

A bird fluttered past and landed on a low branch hanging out over the water. The bird was pale blue and cooed in a soft singsong pattern. Maybe it was one of the ones that glowed in the dark. I remembered all the pictures I'd seen of sharp-beaked birds on the Net. This one cocked its head and looked right at me before it took flight and skimmed just above the creek's gurgling surface.

I walked over to one of the trees and plucked a ripe

piece of my new favorite fruit, then sat down and leaned against the tree trunk. My ankle felt a little better after the cold soak, and the swelling had gone down. As I bit into the juicy goodness, I knew that being able to ingest things other than gel would never get old. The fruit was scrumptious but would taste even better served alongside a slow-roasted tooth monster.

The sound of running snapped me out of my food reverie. I spun around to find James racing toward me from across the camp. He didn't even stop to acknowledge Alec or Markus.

"About time you showed up, *amigo*," Alec called after him.

James didn't slow down until he reached me under the tree. He crouched and shrugged off his pack. "I'm so sorry. I got away as soon as I could. . . . What the . . . ?" His hand touched my cheek. "What happened to your face?"

I'd forgotten how hideous I must look until his eyes focused on my cheek. My heart raced at the nearness of him. "Tooth monster. Long story."

James dug inside his pack for something. "I feel awful. I should have been with you." He pulled out a thin, cylindrical contraption and turned it on. A low hum and blue light emanated from it as he lifted it toward my cheek.

"Wait!" I grabbed his wrist in alarm, remembering the pain that the energetic stitching device had caused Kale.

"It's okay. It won't hurt, I promise." His deep, gravelly voice soothed me at the same time that it made my pulse jump. "It just eradicates all bacteria to avoid infection and causes the cells to regenerate and heal almost instantly. I used this on your rib injury on Earth while you were out cold. You'll still be sore for a while though."

I pulled back from him. "Will it make it go away entirely, like it never happened?"

James had a quizzical look on his face. "No, you'll still have faint lines where the claw marks were. Why, you want scars?"

Relieved, I stepped closer again. "I don't mind them. They remind you what you've survived."

I remembered the scar I'd seen on his lower back in the bunker. James lifted my chin. "You're pretty tough, you know that?"

My cheek tingled where the tube passed over it. Our bodies were inches apart, and I hoped the hum of the device was loud enough to drown out my heart, which felt like it was going to explode out of my chest. I dared to raise my eyes to his. "You're not so bad yourself." I couldn't help but add, "At least when you're unarmed. Speaking of which, you know that whole explanation you gave me back in the containment center?"

James looked miserable as he turned off the machine. "You mean when I poured my heart out, and you didn't remember a word of it?"

The sensation in my cheek faded to an itch, then disappeared after a few seconds.

Like that was my fault. "Yeah, that one. You're gonna

have to humor me and start over."

James put the tube back in his bag. "I will, but I have to give the condensed version for now, because I have something more important to tell you." He grazed my cheek with the back of his hand. His touch sent shivers down my spine. "How does it feel?"

Amazing. "Fine. How's it look?"

James glanced at my cheek. "Perfect. Faint white lines—just what you wanted." He stared deep into my eyes. I couldn't pull my gaze away. "I was a jerk, okay? I thought I could have it both ways. Act like I was following Kale to get the information I wanted and still keep you safe." He ignored my eye roll and continued. "I thought it wouldn't be a big deal to shoot you because I knew it wouldn't be lethal. It was the stupidest thing I've ever done." His hand trailed down my cheek to my neck. "You probably don't want to ever trust me again, but I promise you that I'll spend the rest of my life trying to convince you why you should."

His fingers traced the outline of my jaw, and I fought the torrent of feelings rushing through me. Just when I thought he might try to kiss me again, something flashed across his face and he pulled back. "Look, the reason I ran here wasn't just to check on you."

I could tell from his tone that I didn't want to hear what was coming next. I took a deep breath. "Okay, what?"

He looked down at the ground. "The person that Kale said needed medical attention . . . It was your dad."

Chapter ELEVEN

I COULDN'T EVEN COMPREHEND WHAT JAMES WAS SAYING. "You're saying my dad is the leader of the Resistance?" I knew he'd had a lot of people helping him build our bunker and transport materials back and forth to the pod city, but I'd just thought people respected his intellect.

"Or was, anyway," James said, nodding. He swallowed and took my hands in his. "Your dad's in rough shape, Tora, and not just from withdrawal."

My breath caught in my throat. "What do you mean?"

James' face was grim. "After you escaped with Alec, they . . . they . . ."

Time felt like it stood still. "Just tell me."

"They played on the fact that he knew you were alive. Your dad told us that they put you in the room next to his and tortured you. All he heard through the walls was screaming. He said the agony in your voice was unbearable."

"But it wasn't me." I felt sick to my stomach for whoever had been tortured in my name.

"I told him that, but he's not all there right now."

"Those freakin' burners." Tears leaked from my eyes.

James shook his head. "He's still pretty incoherent. I gave him some meds and I'll go back later to check on him."

"I'm going with you," I said loudly.

"She's going where with you?" Alec called out. "Come up here and tell us what's going on."

James helped me up the embankment toward the camp. "She's not going anywhere," he said.

"Like hell I'm not."

"You're limping," James said matter-of-factly.

I tried to walk normally. "It's fine. I just twisted it a little. No big deal."

James made me sit while he taped up my foot and ankle, then gave me a vial of something to control the inflammation. Markus was on the ground, Lucy's head in his lap while he stroked her fur. Guess she was growing on him a little. He raised an eyebrow at me. "What's goin' on, sweetcakes?"

James and I filled them in on the little we knew.

A look of worry crossed Alec's face. "That means Kale knows you're alive. Your dad doesn't know your history with Kale and would probably have told him how happy he was that you had escaped the containment center."

"That's exactly what happened," James confirmed.

"Kale had a few questions for me."

I shot a look at James. "That means you're in trouble, right?"

"Kale's not happy with me right now, but I'm the only medic around. I told him you were here, but that you didn't want any trouble. I told him you were really motivated by your dad being alive."

Fear surged in me, for James more than for myself. I knew what Kale did to traitors. "But you're not safe with him. Now he knows you didn't kill me on that planet."

James spoke carefully. "He thinks I tried, though. I told him that I really thought you were dead. I said the Consulate must have used heroic efforts to save you because they needed someone who could fire the weapons. That they must have thought your dad was a lost cause, and would never turn over intel about the weapons, so they were focusing on you instead."

"Kale must think the opposite," said Markus, looking at me. "He thinks you're the lost cause, so he's focused on your dad."

I sighed. "Oh, what tangled webs we weave . . ."

Alec grunted. "No way is that burner getting another chance at you, Tora. You stay here with us. We'll protect you."

I laughed. "Great. We'll just hide out in a hut for the rest of our lives . . . or until the Consulate finds us. No thanks. If I wanted that kind of life, I'd go hang out back in the bunker on Earth again."

"That's better than no life, *ángel*," Alec argued.

James gritted his teeth. "Stop calling her that already. Her name is Tora."

Alec folded his arms across his chest. "Like I'd ever forget the name of the *ángel* who rescued me from certain death in Sector Two. I'll call her what I want. At least I follow through on my promises to her."

James took a step toward Alec with his fist clenched. "I'm going to shut you up if you can't do it yourself—that's a promise I know I can keep."

"All right, take it easy, boys," Markus said. He pushed himself up from the dirt while Lucy ran over to Alec. "How 'bout we figure this out in a way that doesn't make Tora want to shoot you both?"

James took a deep breath and uncurled his fist. "You're right. This is stupid." He turned to me. "And Alec's right that it's too dangerous. I don't know what Kale will do, even if your dad is in the room . . . Kale's a little drunk on power right now. You heard him at the bar. He said he has more recruits in other colonies. Who knows what he told them."

I was furious. "He's probably glad Dad is too incapacitated to take charge." A thought hit me. "Wait, did any of you know that my dad was the Resistance leader?"

"No," Alec and James said together. Lucy peered up at me with her innocent puppy-dog eyes. Shame she was the only one I totally trusted.

James must have noticed I looked unconvinced. "I

swear," he said. "Kale said he was shocked himself."

I actually believed that. He wouldn't have tried so hard to kill me if he'd known my relationship with his boss.

Markus stared down at the ground. *No freakin' way.* "Markus?"

He wouldn't meet my eyes. "Aw, hell, Tora, your dad made me swear I wouldn't tell you. He thought it would put you in even more danger if you knew. Then he died— or I thought he died—and I figured it wouldn't do much good to bring it up."

Pissed off didn't even begin to describe how I felt. "God, Markus, how could you not tell me something like that? Don't you think the Resistance would have tried to save me if they knew I was the daughter of their leader? But no, you didn't want anyone else to know just so you could make a buck off the weapons." I thought of all the trips Markus had taken to and from the pod city and how Dad had trusted him more than anyone else. Markus would have known exactly what my dad was doing.

I glared at the group and focused on Markus. "Can we all agree that no one keeps any more secrets from anyone else?"

"Yes," Markus grumbled.

"Of course. I trust you with my life," said Alec.

James stayed remarkably silent. *Figured.*

Tree branches snapped behind us, and we scrambled for our weapons.

Sonya trudged into the clearing. "Keep your pants on.

It's just us." She was followed closely by Reed and the two guards I'd seen earlier.

"Hey—Trent, Ian, I haven't seen you in ages," Markus said.

Trent shook his hand. "We've seen you plenty, man. Just not sober. Good to see you looking better."

Markus shrugged. "Thanks, I'm trying."

Reed flashed me a smile. "We just wanted to make sure you were okay after Kale almost saw you in the bar."

Sonya rolled her eyes. "No, *she* wanted to make sure you were okay." She fixed her eyes on James. "I wanted to know what the plan is now that Kale's back."

James eyed her. "So you're still on our side?"

Sonya sighed. "Depends what side you're talking about. What's going on?"

I still didn't trust Sonya at all, and I wondered how much James would say. His face looked guarded when he spoke. "We're figuring out our next moves now that Tora's dad is here." He studied Sonya's face as if to gauge her reaction.

"Tora's dad is the leader of the Resistance?" Sonya arched an eyebrow, like she couldn't quite believe it. I wanted to punch her.

"Wow, that's so cool," said Reed. "Oh wait, he needed medical attention, right? Is he okay?"

"He will be," said James. "He just needs some time."

Trent cleared his throat and looked at James. "Ian and I wanted to let you know that we're with you, whatever you decide to do. Kale's so hell bent on revenge against the Consulate that he can't see straight."

Ian nodded his head. "He's a little too much like the Consulate now, if you ask me. I think you should stay leader, James. There are many of us who agree."

"Mutiny," Sonya smirked. "I like it. Things were getting a little too boring around here for my taste anyway. As long as we get to take down the Consulate, I'll be happy."

"Gotta be honest. Revolution scares the crap out of me but, of course, I'm with you guys," Reed said. "What do we do now?" The more she spoke, the more her vulnerability and sweetness reminded me of Callie. It made me wonder if I had even a drop of sweetness left, myself.

James looked deep in thought. "Kale called an emergency command meeting two light breaks from now. He said there's news about a Consulate attack—wants to give orders to his soldiers."

Trent stroked his chin. "That works . . . it's before our regularly scheduled meeting. We can find out what Kale knows and then make a plan."

James looked at me. "That means your dad will be alone while Kale's heading that first meeting."

"I take it he's nearby since you got back so fast?"

James nodded. "Yes, he's in a solo encampment on the other side of the bar. We'll all attend the meeting while you go see him."

I could have sworn a look of triumph flashed across Sonya's face. She'd get to spend time with James while I was gone. It barely registered, though. All I could focus on was seeing Dad again. Hopefully, he was doing better after some medical attention.

Markus had been pretty quiet and I noticed his eyes on Sonya. Great. It would be just like him to go after the girl I couldn't stand.

"Hey, Markus," I said. He broke his attention away from Sonya. "Will you be able to get past the bar? Do you need another dose of the withdrawal med?"

He stretched his arms over his head. "No, I'm good. It must have been pretty powerful stuff 'cause all I'm craving right now is some roasted monster meat."

"Good," I said. My stomach rumbled and hunger gnawed at me. "And I second the idea of monster meat."

Trent and Ian powered up their weapons. "All right," Ian said. "Let's get to hunting."

Everyone sat around the fire, laughing and sharing stories. Trent was smart and insightful, while Ian seemed a little more rough around the edges.

Reed came over and sat by me. "Can I braid your hair?"

My hand flew up to my frizzy, jungle-woman hair. "Does it look that bad?"

Reed laughed. "No, silly. I just want to. My sisters and I used to do this with each other all the time. Turn around." As her hands worked through my hair, I remembered a time when I was five or six and we lived in the pod city. My mom had said she wanted to brush my hair, and she'd worked my out-of-control curls into soft waves. It was the last time she ever did that. Tears came to my eyes and I brushed them away.

Alec asked Reed a lot of questions while she did my hair. I'd lost my sister, but Reed had lost all three of hers. When she finished, she took a long piece of grass and tied it around the end of the braid. "Ta da!" she exclaimed.

James smiled. "Even more gorgeous than you were already."

Sonya snapped a twig between her fingers. I'm sure in her mind, I was that twig.

Reed went to sit by Alec, and they resumed their conversation. She was so animated when she spoke, and Alec seemed transfixed. The word that popped into my head was "cute."

"So Sonya, have we met before?" Markus asked.

I groaned inside. It was his way of asking if they'd slept together.

She eyed him and tossed her red hair. "No. In fact, I'm pretty sure I'm one of the few girls you haven't 'met'."

Anyone else would have been embarrassed, but Markus just laughed. "What's a girl like you look for in a guy, anyway?"

This was not happening. James must have sensed my annoyance and squeezed my hand.

Sonya stared at Markus across the fire as she twirled another twig in her hand. "Aside from sobriety? What any girl wants, I guess. Don't get me wrong—I don't need a man, and am doing fine on my own, but it would be nice for someone to sweep me off my feet. Someone who is strong yet romantic, and isn't afraid to express what he feels." Her eyes briefly flicked to James. "Somehow, that appears impossible to find."

"Guess you haven't met the right man yet, then," Markus said matter-of-factly. He was oblivious to the daggers I was shooting at him.

Sonya shrugged and tossed the twig into the flames. "Guess not."

Markus shook me awake shortly before the second light break. "Wake up, sweetcakes. We gotta get moving."

Though I'd agreed to share his hut even though I'd had my doubts, he had been a perfect gentleman. The monster meat I'd eaten had put me into a food coma, and I'd slept like the dead. Reed and the others had left after the meal, and I'd been relieved when Markus didn't make any more moves on Sonya. Alec, on the other hand, had seemed very taken with Reed and they didn't seem to want to say goodbye. Between Alec and Markus, at least one of them had good taste.

We stepped outside into the dark. My ankle felt surprisingly good. The wrap and meds had worked wonders. Alec secured Lucy inside his hut and gave her a huge tooth-monster bone for a snack. "Stay, girl, we'll be back soon."

James had taken off after our meal to attend to Dad.

I knew Dad was in good hands, but selfishly wished that James' hands could be in two places at once.

The sky had completely cleared and the moons and stars glowed above us. I pointed upward. "Look, there's the Weeping Boy."

"You remembered," Alec said, clearly pleased.

Markus looked at us. "Huh?"

"Alec named a constellation." I showed Markus the stars as we trekked toward the command center. James would meet us in the woods near the bar and take me to Dad before joining Alec and Markus at the meeting.

The air was cool, yet mild, and energy surged through me. Maybe it was the combo of meat and sleep, but I felt fantastic. We walked along the creek in contented silence for a while.

"This is much easier without having to hide from a storm under the trees," I remarked.

Alec clucked his tongue. "Never do that again. The light flashes can kill you if they hit a tree."

"Now you tell me. Guess I was more worried about everything else that could kill me."

Our pace sped up as the sky lightened. I couldn't wait to see Dad. He'd know I was okay, and then he'd pull through.

We soon reached the bar area and waited near the clearing. I grew antsy. Where was James?

Sunlight streaked across the sky in pink and orange blazes. "You guys go ahead," I said to Markus and Alec.

"It's almost full light and you can't be late for the meeting. I want to know everything Kale says."

"Sorry, sweetcakes, we're not leaving you." Markus cracked a smile. "Mainly because I know your temper and I'd never hear the end of it if something happened after I left you. Also, James might kill me."

Branches crackled nearby, and James broke through a cluster of trees. "Okay, not much time," he said breathlessly. "You two, get to the meeting. Tora, this way."

Markus saluted and ran off with Alec toward the command center. I tried to keep up with James as we tore across the clearing to the woods on the other side of the bar. My ankle started to remind me why it was wrapped in the first place. I'd have to work through the pain because I'd never been in this section of the forest before.

My lungs burned and my ankle throbbed, but I managed to keep James in sight. Finally, he stopped and put his hands on his knees to catch his breath. I reached him and he pointed into the woods. "Go straight that way for about another quarter mile and you'll find the hut where your dad is." He placed his hands on my shoulders in a gentle but firm manner. "No matter what, don't stay longer than twenty minutes. Get back to the other side of the bar and don't stop until you get to your hut. Okay, I gotta go."

"Will I see you later?" I blurted. God, that sounded pathetic.

"Yes, when it's dark." James turned and ran back to the command center.

The trees stretched out before me, and I hoped I was moving in the right direction. I ran as quickly as possible, dodging tree limbs. Had James meant no more than twenty minutes with my dad or from the time he left for the meeting? And how the hell was I supposed to track time out here anyway?

I almost stumbled into the hut before I noticed it—it was covered by thick shrubs. This wasn't like the other encampments. There was only the one hut and it was set between two large trees. If I hadn't been looking for it, I probably would have walked right past it. Even though I knew Kale should be at the meeting, I hesitated and listened outside the entrance flap. Labored breathing was all I heard, so I pulled the flap back and peered inside. Dad was alone, tucked away on a cot near the back wall.

"Dad?" I whispered as I crossed the small space.

When he didn't answer, I shook him gently and called out louder. "Dad!"

At this rate, it would take the twenty minutes just to wake him. He stirred and mumbled something that sounded like my name. I shook him harder. "It's me, Tora. You have to wake up."

Dad opened his eyes, which widened when he saw me. He reached out a hand to touch the fabric of my T-shirt. "You're real," he croaked.

I took his hand and squeezed it. "Yes, Dad, I'm real."

"But . . . but I heard them kill you." His voice broke. "They promised that if I cooperated they would spare you, but they didn't." Confusion blanketed his face.

"It wasn't me. Alec got me out, and I've been with the Resistance in Callie City. I don't know who that was in the containment center but I'm fine. I promise."

He reached up, and I pulled him into a hug. "It's okay," I said into his shoulder. "Now we just need to get you strong again."

"I remember when you were a little girl back in the pod city. Callie was a baby, and you were holding her in your arms. She kept reaching up toward your face with her tiny hand, and you gave her these slobbery kisses on the back of her hand that made both of you laugh so hard." Dad's eyes filled with tears. "I don't think I've seen you that happy since then." His arms gripped me tightly. "I'm so sorry, please forgive me."

I pulled back a little and grasped his hands in mine. "Don't be sorry, I'm fine. This isn't your fault."

"No." He shook his head. "That's not what I meant." His voice cracked again and I gave him some water that was set on the floor by the cot.

He took a long sip and cleared his throat. "They told me they would stop hurting you if I helped them with the formulas to rekey the guns. They'd somehow found out you were the only one who could fire them. I couldn't bear to listen to you being hurt." Dad's voice, though quiet, was a little stronger. "So I helped them, but then they killed you—or killed someone—anyway. I'm sure they were about to kill me too, when Kale and his men broke in and rescued me."

So Kale had saved my dad from certain death. He'd wanted nothing but to kill me, yet had risked his life to save Dad's. I couldn't figure that burner out.

Dad buried his head in his hands. "I'm so ashamed."

A sinking feeling took hold of my stomach and the air went out of my lungs. "Why, Dad? How did you help them?"

He sighed and took a sheet of thermoplastic paper from inside his shirt. It looked like it had been removed from a notebook, like the stack I'd burned outside the bunker on Earth. He pressed it into my hand. "Don't show this to anyone. It's the formulas to rekey the weapons. They didn't get this—I hid it inside the pad of my cot. But . . ." His eyes filled with sorrow and pain. "I acted like I was going along with them and wrote down some of the equations. Not all of the ones in your hand—I left out a few key steps—but the blueprints are there, nonetheless."

I knew what that meant before he continued. It was what I'd tried so hard to prevent.

Dad shook his head. "With a little fine-tuning, they'll know how to rekey the triggers. Anyone will be able to use the guns."

Chapter TWELVE

I SWALLOWED HARD AND TRIED TO KEEP THE HORROR I FELT hidden as I tucked the paper into my pants. If the Consulate found the weapons before I did and rekeyed them, then any of those burners could fire them. They could be used against anyone who disagreed with the government. There wouldn't be a Resistance anymore.

"I'm sure it will be fine, Dad," I said and patted his hand in reassurance. "Kale has the guns and I'm sure they're safe for now."

"What? Kale didn't tell me he had the guns."

I wasn't sure how much to tell Dad. He was in no shape to stand up to Kale. If Dad knew Kale had stolen the guns and had ordered me killed, he would likely end up dead himself. A bird twittered outside the hut, reminding me how little time I had left. It sounded like the same kind of bird I'd heard earlier.

"So why did Kale save you, Dad? Because you're the Resistance leader?"

He let out a long breath. "You found out. When I figured out that the Consulate planned to use the guns to kill people for their W.A.R. machines I enlisted others to help me move the weapons. We had a few meetings. One thing led to another and, next thing I know, I'm leading the Resistance. Soon after, most of my confidantes were murdered by the Consulate, so I decided it was safer to lead remotely. I only knew Kale through the com system, but he's been so supportive, and I can't believe he risked his life for me."

My throat tightened. "You don't think he had ulterior motives for saving you?"

Dad took another sip of water and lowered his voice. "Well, it sounds like he's taken the Resistance in a slightly different direction than what I'd intended. I simply wanted to stop the Consulate and let the people rule themselves. Kale started out that way, but now I think he wants to destroy the Consulate for good. After what I've been through in the past year, I'm not sure I blame him."

I sighed. If Dad only knew how ruthless Kale really was, he'd be horrified. Dad was weak, and I wanted to drag him out of this hut and bring him back to our camp where I could tell him the truth. But when Kale found the hut empty, he'd know for sure that James was involved and wouldn't hesitate to kill him. I'd let Dad get a little stronger, and then figure out how to get him away from Kale.

I chose my next words carefully. "I think you're right about Kale changing. Be careful around him, Dad . . . and don't mention that I was here."

He wouldn't let go of my hand. "I just can't believe you're alive."

The paper moved inside my waistband. "Why did you bring the formulas with you to that meeting?" I asked.

Dad sighed. "To protect you. I knew that meeting was probably a setup. If they ever found our bunker and the weapons, they would have turned the place upside down. They would have found my notebooks and discovered the equations, anyway. It was a risk taking the formulas. The Consulate soldiers could have found them on me before I was able to hide them, but I had to take that chance to protect you."

I thought of the notebooks I'd destroyed. The information would have gone up in flames if he'd left them with me. Problem solved. "Why not get rid of the formulas rather than hide them?"

He shrugged. "I should have. I know that now. But I thought there might be a time when they'd be needed. The technology was the biggest weapons breakthrough of the century, so maybe it was part ego that I couldn't bring myself to destroy my work"

The bird tweeted again, a lilting, melodic sound. I was running out of time.

"I have to go, Dad, but I'll be back soon. When you're feeling up to it, you can come stay with us." I hugged him tightly, as if it were the last time I'd get the chance. I thought of Callie and how I'd give anything for one more hug from her.

"You be careful too," he said. "And hurry back when you can."

I kissed his cheek and ran back into the woods. Remembering my gun, I pulled it out and fired another test shot. The laser exploded through the nearest tree and left a gaping hole. Nice. The gun had finally dried out. I tucked it away again and patted it against my side. A functional gun provided a strange sense of comfort.

There were still a solid few hours of light left, and I let up on my pace when I neared the bar with no sign of Kale. I didn't know what to do with the lethal formulas Dad had given me. It's not like I'd ever be reprogramming the weapons; I'd just be destroying them. The meeting must still be going strong. I darted across the clearing in front of the bar.

"Psst, Tora, over here!"

I whipped around. Reed stood outside the bar, by the corner, gun in hand.

"Hey, Reed, what are you doing?" I asked. "Why aren't you at the meeting?"

"Ugh, I can't stand political talk," she said as she motioned me over. "Besides, I'm helping as a lookout while Trent and Ian are inside. It's more important that they know what's going on. Not that I love having to hold this." She lifted the gun in disgust.

I smiled. She was totally perfect for Alec—if we all lived long enough.

A small insect with bright green wings dipped and dove between us. For a second, it hovered over Reed's shoulder and I thought it might land on her, but then it zipped away again.

I peered beyond Reed toward the command center. James' warning echoed in my head. "I can't stay."

"I know, it's just that I overheard Sonya talking about the guns on the way to the meeting," Reed said. "I was going to tell James as soon as I saw him. I mean, she'll probably tell him anyway since she's on our side."

Goose bumps broke out on my arms. "What exactly did she say?"

Reed pushed a lock of her hair back with the barrel of the gun. "She said something like 'the Consulate doesn't stand a chance after the ammo I just saw.' I guess Kale showed it to her."

My heart leapt into my throat. It's not likely that Kale had whisked Sonya off to another planet and back without anyone noticing, which meant that the guns had to be somewhere nearby.

"Did she say anything else?" I asked.

Reed shook her head. "She was talking to Kale's pilot. I didn't want to be too obvious. They were walking past me."

The fact that I was so close to finding out the location of the guns made me giddy. My ankle wasn't even bothering me anymore.

Loud voices pierced the serenity of the forest and branches snapped as a stampede of footsteps came from the direction of the bar. The meeting must have let out and the obvious place to discuss things was over a drink. *Crap.*

Without a word, I darted into the trees and hoped no one had seen me, especially Kale. I rushed along the creek back toward camp. The scent of wildflowers drifted through the trees but I didn't dare stop to pick any. By the time I reached camp, my run had morphed into a haphazard jog. My breathing was ragged as I dove into Markus' hut.

Lucy ran in and jumped all over me. I eased her down. "Shhh, we have to be quiet," I said as though she could understand me. She understood something though, because she circled around in place and lay down at my side.

I stroked her soft fur and tried to catch my breath again. I didn't even want to think about what would happen if Kale returned with the guys. Since he knew I was still alive, he'd have to figure I was with Markus and Alec. Kale was a jerk, but not a dumb one. I sat on the cot with my arms huddled around my legs, then remembered the paper in my waistband and shoved it under the cot just in case.

A plan formed in my mind. After we located the bio-weapons, I'd have James and the others help me take care of Kale and his men, then we'd unload the guns in space and get on with our lives. Preferably a little closer to the beach. I'd like a water view. *Great plan, but what about the Consulate?* Everything always led back to the Consulate.

Voices broke my reverie and I strained to hear who was coming. My shoulders relaxed when I recognized the voices as friendly ones. I peered out of the hut. "I'm in here. Just keeping Lucy company."

Lucy bounded out and licked Alec's hand. Markus and James were with him.

James grabbed my arm. "You scared me back there when I saw you with Reed. I thought Kale would see you. C'mon, I want to tell you about the meeting."

James pulled me into the hut and secured the flap behind us. I stepped away from him and crossed my arms over my chest. Running from Kale was not something I wanted to keep doing. I'd have to deal with him sooner rather than later, but before I could say anything to James, his mouth was on mine. My words dissolved. James ran his hands slowly down my still-crossed arms, gently pulling them to my sides, then wove our fingers together as his lips moved against mine. After a minute, he broke away.

He cupped my face with his hands. "Look, I know you want the guns. We just have to be careful how we go about things. You have your dad to worry about now, and according to Kale, there will probably be a Consulate attack within the week."

I sighed. "But why do I have to keep out of sight? Kale knows I'm here anyway."

James took his hand from my face and ran it through

his hair. "Yeah, but the game changed since he found out your dad was alive. I'm trying to figure things out. I don't know what that means for you . . . could be good, could be bad."

I wanted to tell James my plan, but part of me was afraid he'd think it was stupid. Maybe he'd play along. I took a deep breath. "Speaking of figuring things out, I have an idea now that Markus is sober and all . . ."

"Is this the part where I tell you that I can hear everything going on in there?" Markus called out. "Don't get me wrong, it's been an entertaining few minutes, but shouldn't I get to know what your plans for 'sober Markus' are?"

Leaving the tent meant no more kissing, but Markus was right. And I didn't want any future kissing to include Markus' presence in the vicinity. I strode past James and spoke in a low voice. "Don't think that this means that you're forgiven. You have more work to do on that front."

A rare smile flickered across James' face. "Don't worry. I've got a lot of work planned for later."

I raised an eyebrow. "What does that mean?"

He waved me through the flap. "Patience isn't one of your strong suits. You know that, right?"

I marched outside and dull pain shot through my ankle. "I think I've been more patient than you deserve. Lucky for you, I've become more forgiving since I first met you."

"Too forgiving, if you ask me," Alec remarked as Lucy tried to push a stick into his hand.

Markus stared at Alec. "Are you kidding me? I'm all for anyone that gets this girl to chill out."

I plopped down by the fire pit and unwound the wrap from my ankle. No swelling and the pain was little more than a pain-in-the-ass ache. James pulled out a new wrap but I waved it away. "One more dose of the anti-inflammatory med and I should be good."

Markus grinned at me while James pressed the tip of the vial to my ankle. "So, what's your grand plan, sweetcakes?"

The med worked instantly. I wiggled my foot. "Basically, we get my dad away from Kale, find the guns, kill Kale . . . and his men if needed. Then we dump the guns and go from there."

No one said anything for a minute.

Markus spoke first. "Um, so, is that like the bare bones version of the plan, or is there a more elaborate version?"

James spoke carefully. "That's a start, but you have to understand that the goal of the Resistance has always been to take out the Consulate." I could see the wheels turning in his head. "And if the Consulate is planning an attack, we don't stand a chance at the moment."

I knew what he meant. We didn't stand a chance without Dad's guns.

Alec tossed the stick to Lucy. "Why stay if it means certain war? Whether it's Kale or the Consulate, we're not safe here. Why not just leave and start over? We can do it if we stick together." He looked at me carefully. "And that way, you wouldn't have to kill people. I thought that was the whole reason you wanted to get rid of the guns anyway."

He was right. I'd never wanted to kill anyone . . . but since the Consulate imprisoned Dad, then tortured and killed someone they claimed was me, I was starting to reconsider my position.

"I love the idea of our group sticking together. Maybe we should all hold hands and sing a little song."

"Be serious, Markus," I said. "Besides, how hard was it to find a planet like this, with water everywhere . . . and oxygen? We shouldn't have to give it up to run away from Consulate burners just because they want to kill us." I pointed at James. "You named this place after my sister. Hell if I'm leaving."

Alec gave Lucy a pat on the head. "I'm clearly the only one here who is being serious. This isn't a game. It's not funny."

I put my hand on my hip. "I'm sorry, Alec. Is my plan funny to you?"

"That's not what I meant. I just think we need to be rational here and not make decisions based purely on emotion." He stared pointedly from me to James.

Now I was pissed. "Seriously? Like how I rescued you from Sector Two . . . because no rational person would have done that."

Alec grabbed the stick from Lucy and tossed it farther away.

Markus chuckled. "She's got a point. I thought she

was a little crazy myself when she suggested it, but then I thought, what the hell. And you wouldn't be here at all if it weren't for her. So who's the one being emotional, *amigo?*"

Alec looked like he wanted to punch someone, but clamped his mouth shut. He knew Markus was right. He'd told me repeatedly how he owed me his life.

The sky would start to dim soon, and I wanted to figure this out before dark. Lucy brought back the stick to Markus instead of Alec. She'd apparently sensed his anger.

James spoke in measured tones. "Okay, what about a plan that accomplishes what everybody wants?"

My head snapped up to look at him. If he ever wanted to kiss me again, he'd go along with what I wanted. "Excuse me?"

James held his hands out palms up. "I know it's not exactly what you planned—but Alec has a point." James rushed on before I could say anything. "I love the idea of getting your dad and the guns. I'm all in for that. My concern is attempting to protect him while fighting Kale and his men at the same time. We don't even know for sure how many of the Resistance are loyal to him. And, honestly, I don't see how we can beat the Consulate without using your dad's weapons."

I crossed my arms. "So, after we get the guns and Dad, we just leave? We give up?"

"No," James said as he touched my leg. "It would just be temporary. We'd go to a colony on a nearby planet with the guns to regroup and give your dad time to get stronger.

In the meantime, we'd let false info slip to the Consulate that the guns are right here in Callie City."

Markus laughed loudly. "That's freakin' brilliant. The Consulate would do the job for us. They'd destroy Kale and everyone who's associated with him."

Alec looked thoughtful, then nodded. "And after all that, the Consulate still wouldn't have the guns. I love it. It's a quiet revolution, a smart one that won't involve mass deaths." I wondered if he was thinking about Reed.

I considered what James had said for a minute. "And then we come back?"

James shrugged "The Consulate would think there's nothing left here. I doubt they'd return if they believed the Resistance was wiped out."

"What about the others who don't support Kale? I don't want them to die."

"They won't," said James. "We'll take them with us."

It almost sounded like this could work. "But what about the Resistance? You said their mission was to take down the Consulate."

Alec shrugged. "It is. But I bet between James and me, we could convince them why this is the best way . . . for now." I could see in his eyes that he hadn't totally abandoned getting revenge at some point.

I eyed Markus. "You said you left your ship here when you rode to Earth on Kale's to steal my guns. Does that old bird still fly?"

Markus had the decency to look ashamed. "Yeah, she's

fine now . . . I fixed her up when we got here. I keep her covered with brush and leaves so she won't be spotted by the Consulate."

"And James, you know where the guns are, right?" I asked.

James looked confused. "No, why would I?"

Without the location of the guns, this plan was dead in the water. I needed those weapons. "Reed said Kale showed them to Sonya, so I assumed you knew where they were too."

James let out a low whistle. "Sonya said she had something to tell me after the meeting, but Kale was still with us, and then I saw you. Either way, the fact that Kale didn't tell me about the guns means he definitely doesn't trust me anymore."

I shook my head. "Or it means that Sonya might not be as on board with us as we thought."

Alec cleared his throat. "Sonya seems rather fond of James. I bet that's what she was going to tell him. Maybe he can get the location out of her . . ."

I didn't want James getting anything out of her. "Maybe Reed could find out, like, spy for us?" The moment the words left my mouth, I felt guilty. Reed shouldn't endanger herself just because I couldn't stand Sonya.

"Reed seems really nice," said Markus. "Is it possible that she and I . . . you know?"

"No way," Alec said. "She's too sweet for you."

"Thanks a lot."

I turned to James. "Part of why I can't figure out where the guns are is that Kale's actions aren't making sense to me. Why would he save my dad?"

James scratched the stubble on his chin. "Kale's so power hungry now. It doesn't make sense that he found out the leader of the Resistance was alive and took heroic efforts to rescue him. He likes being the leader too much."

Alec looked up at the darkening sky and threw some logs into the fire pit. His face had softened, maybe into resignation, and he looked thoughtful. "Your dad must have something that Kale needs. It's not the guns, so what else could he have that Kale wants?"

The truth slammed into me like a ton of meat monster. "The formulas."

James' eyes widened. Markus frowned and asked, "What are you talking about?"

"That's it," James said. "The equations to rekey the weapons. Then Kale and all his soldiers can fire them." He looked at me. "Don't worry. Your dad would never give those up to Kale."

I gulped and looked down at the ground. "Maybe not, but he gave them to the Consulate."

Chapter THIRTEEN

ALL EYES WERE ON ME. A BRISK WIND KICKED UP AS THE SUN lost its grasp of the horizon and a deep gray settled over us. Alec lit the fire and tossed a handful of twigs on top for good measure. He glanced at me like he wanted to say something but bit his lip instead. Markus just gaped at me.

I didn't want them to judge Dad, because I would have done the same exact thing if the situation was reversed, and I thought the Consulate was hurting him. "When I saw Dad, he told me he gave the equations to the Consulate officials back in the containment center when he thought they were torturing me. He didn't give them all the formulas, but he gave them enough to eventually figure out the rest."

"Well, that's a crap load of hell right there."

I sighed. "Always helpful, Markus. Thanks."

James stood by the fire and snapped a twig in his hands.

"We have to find those guns fast . . . and get your dad away from Kale as quickly as possible."

"I agree, but he's still so weak."

James came and sat by my side. "I know, but I'll give him stronger meds next time and then I'll find out where the guns are."

"Speaking of guns and burners," I said. "What exactly did Kale say about the Consulate, anyway?"

Alec looked grim in the firelight. "Kale spoke of 'imminent danger' and said a Consulate attack is coming any day now. It's hard to know what's real and what he's saying just to get people to do what he wants."

Markus studied the flames. "Fear is a hell of a motivator. It sounded real though."

James nodded. "I agree. Which means he'll likely put pressure on your dad about the gun formulas. . . . That's why Kale wants me to get him better so quickly. He told me he wanted your dad 'fixed' by the time he comes back."

Alec watched me across the fire. "Kale said he's leaving at first light break tomorrow. He's bringing a few recruits from a nearby moon but will be back by the second light break."

I frowned, not understanding what Alec meant by "tomorrow" until I remembered the grooves that marked days on the timekeeping device at the bar.

James spoke slowly. "That gives us about eight hours to locate the guns, get your dad, and get out of here."

My heart leapt in my throat, but I had to play it cool.

I stared directly ahead and watched the flames lick the edges of the twigs. "Does that mean we have a plan?"

James spoke in a low voice. "Of course." He turned to Markus and Alec. "Gentlemen?"

Markus twirled a larger twig back and forth between his fingers. "Sure, but can some of the other people we bring along be of the female variety? It'd be a shame to leave all the good ones here."

I scoffed. "I bet you can't even name a single girl who has had the pleasure of your company these past few months."

Markus shot me a wounded look over the flames. "I'm offended. Of course I can, there was a Sara in there somewhere I think, and . . . a Becca, definitely a Becca. Come to think of it, they might have both been there together."

Alec's face darkened. "I'd treat a woman so much better than that. She'd be the only name I remembered."

"That's touching," said Markus, tossing the twig on the ground. "But sometimes it's nice to have something other than a little fire to keep you warm at night."

A meat monster howled in the darkness and Alec leapt to his feet. "I'll go hunt. I'm hungry."

"Want help?" Markus asked. He didn't look like he had any intention of getting up.

Alec pulled out his gun and powered it up. "No, I'm *bueno*. Need some alone time."

"Suit yourself," said Markus as he stretched his legs out in front of the fire.

James had shifted closer to me and, without thinking, I moved my body several inches toward his.

I thought about everything we had to accomplish in the next few light breaks. And people I wanted to bring with us, like Reed. James would know who else would be good to have as allies, and Markus had a whole curvy guest list in mind. "Your ship isn't that big, Markus. How will we fit everyone?" I asked.

"Hey," Markus protested. "Watch how you talk about a man's ship. It's not the size that matters, it's how well it holds up under pressure."

"Max has his own ship," James interjected. "He'd come with us. I'm sure of it."

I watched James. "Have you thought about this before?"

"Yeah, when Kale returned with your dad, I started planning how to keep you both safe."

Luckily it had grown dark enough to hide the blush I felt rising up my cheeks.

The carcass of the animal lay stripped of meat, and I licked my lips. Hopefully, the next planet would have meat monsters too, because I was getting used to this.

Markus belched and yawned. "Time for some shut-eye. We only have two light breaks before Kale leaves and I need me some rest."

"Good idea," said Alec. "I think probably we all could use some sleep."

"James!" a voice whispered from the woods. "James!"

Sonya emerged from the trees, her hair wild and eyes bright. Markus stopped mid-step and stared at her as though entranced. She glared at me and looked back at James. "I looked for you in your hut, but should have known you'd be here again. I have something important to tell you."

Part of me was disappointed that I'd been wrong about her. It was easier to dislike someone who was dishonest. But maybe I was about to find out where Dad's weapons were. The thought made me ecstatic.

A sharp cracking sound in the brush right behind us made me jump to my feet. *What if she brought Kale here with her?* I whipped out my gun and aimed into the darkness.

James threw his arm across me and pushed my raised weapon down. I had a sudden flashback of him taking my weapon. *Not once, but twice.* My gut twisted in fear. I snatched my gun out of his reach and backed away.

"Don't shoot. It's just me. Sorry to scare you." Max walked out of the trees toward the fire pit.

"What the—" I said. "Why the hell is everybody sneaking up on us?"

Max smiled. "James asked me to come. Guess he hasn't told you yet?"

I frowned and looked at James. He wasn't smiling. He looked like he'd just been kicked in the stomach. He stared at the ground. "Maybe this wasn't such a good idea after all."

"Nonsense," said Max. "I've got the ship ready and everything. You and Tora are scheduled for departure in five minutes." He watched Lucy chew on a gigantic bone. "Hey, did you guys save any dinner?"

Markus tossed him a rib the size of my forearm. "It's all we got left. Sorry."

"Departure for where?" Sonya demanded. "What's going on?"

Alec took a step closer and his hand inched toward his gun. "I don't remember anything in the plan about taking Tora away."

The old familiar fear gripped hold of my gut, and the hand holding my gun started to shake. "Yeah, what the hell is going on, James?"

He ran his hand through his sandy hair. "I wanted to surprise you with something . . . something good. But I see you're scared. You still don't trust me." He reached for my hand and held it between his.

I tried to ignore the electric jolt that I felt at his touch. "It's not like surprises have been a good thing in my life so far. You of all people should know that."

Sonya stared at my hands in James', her eyes narrowed. I couldn't read the exact emotions on her face but none of them were happy. "Wait, what did you want to tell us? Is it about my dad's guns?" I asked.

Her eyes remained fixed on our interlocked hands. "Nothing as important as whatever you two are doing tonight, I guess. It can wait until our scheduled meeting. Sorry, I shouldn't have come." I could have sworn she had tears in her eyes as she headed back into the woods.

"Sonya, wait—" James started, but she fled into the dark without turning back.

"We should go after her," I said, "and make her tell us." We were so close to finding out the location of the guns.

"We won't find her if she doesn't want to be found," James said. "Let her cool down and I'm sure she'll come through when I meet with her."

"Okay, not that I don't appreciate good drama, but I'm freakin' exhausted." Markus saluted us. "Whatever you're up to, be back on time. Night, kids." He ducked into his hut and Lucy trotted in after him with the huge bone tucked between her teeth.

"No way," Markus yelled from inside. "I don't have many rules, but no bones in the hut is one of them." The bone came hurtling back out. Remarkably, Lucy didn't come chasing after it. She'd curled up with Markus instead. Guess I'd been wrong about her having the best sense of all of us.

I turned back to the others. Alec's eyes gleamed in the firelight. He didn't look happy. He didn't strike me as a guy that liked surprises much, but I could relate. All the surprises that had happened in my life so far had sucked big-time. Still, I was curious.

"I'm not sure about this," I admitted. "Maybe it's not the best time for a surprise."

Max walked in between James and me and grabbed hold of our arms. "You'll have to work this out on the ship. No time to spare. It's cutting it close as it is." He pulled us toward the woods and turned back to Alec. "They'll be safe and sound, and back in two hours. No worries, man."

James was silent as we walked.

"How far is your ship?" I asked Max.

"Not far at all. Just up ahead behind some brush." He jerked his thumb toward James. "You wouldn't believe the trouble this guy went through for you. It had to be at night to avoid Consulate flyovers, had to be in the right window of time, had to be—"

"Okay, Max, I got this." James reached for my hand. I let him take it despite the doubt still gnawing inside me. Trust wasn't a commodity I was used to trading in. I'd been positive I could trust James several times and he'd let me down—hard.

We walked in silence until we reached Max's ship. Max bowed at the hatch door. "My lady," he said and waved me inside. I hadn't known Max long, but I liked him. I was all too aware of my well-worn T-shirt and the tendrils of frizzed hair that had escaped my braid, and knew the chances were slim that I'd ever be called "my lady" again.

I smiled. "Should I take my usual seat?"

He grinned. "Absolutely." Max settled into the pilot's seat and picked up a headset. "Settle back and enjoy the short ride. I'll have this earpiece on so I won't hear any, uh, conversing back there. Ready for takeoff, James?"

James strapped himself in and gave Max a thumbs-up sign. The ship rose into the air. I watched out the dashboard window as we hovered a moment, then sped off toward the dark horizon. Max put on his headset and started moving his head to an unheard rhythm.

I turned to James. "Can you tell me where we're going yet?"

"No, you'll see soon enough." He undid his seat restraint and knelt on the floor at my side. "Look, Tora, I owe you so many apologies that I don't even know where to start. It's just . . . the look on your face back there . . . like you thought I was going to hurt you. I'm not sure that's something I can ever undo."

I gulped. He could be right. "You can try, though. I've heard your explanation but it doesn't take away the fact that you betrayed me . . . multiple times." I thought of the time he'd taken my gun away, then pointed his own at my head. "I just don't understand what you were thinking."

James grasped my hand in his. "I'm sorry. I was cocky. Too cocky. I thought I could manage everything on my own." His eyes searched mine. "I thought I was such a great shot that it would be no problem to shoot you, because I knew you'd live. Except then I didn't. The moment I shot you, I was gripped with crazy worry that I'd actually killed you." His voice broke. "When the Consulate soldiers started shooting at me, I knew I deserved it."

My heart battled with my head as a tear slid out of the corner of my eye. *Dammit.* "But you lived. And I lived, *and* you found out who killed your family, so was it worth it?"

"God, no. That's what I'm trying to tell you." He pressed my hand to his cheek. "You know how I told you about the time Markus first showed me your picture and I couldn't shoot at you when you came out of your bunker that day?"

I nodded. Tons of lasers had come my way, yet James had insisted that he shot everywhere but at me.

James sighed. "There was this sadness in your face in that picture. I recognized the same thing in myself. Then, after I got to know you, I had these feelings for you that I tried to push away. I was so torn between what I felt for you and what I thought I needed to do to avenge my family. The only thing I want now is your forgiveness, but I know I don't deserve it."

The stubble on his face tickled my hand but I couldn't pull away. I wasn't sure if I'd ever be able to pull away from him again. "You're right. You don't deserve it," I said, though I didn't move my hand. "I'll let you try to earn my trust, but I'm not making any promises. And if you ever shoot me again, we're done. A girl has her limits."

James kissed my hand. "No more shooting."

The ship thudded softly against the ground, and James grabbed the side of my chair to keep his balance. Max whipped off his headset and turned around to us. "We've arrived. I'll be right here if you need me. You only have one hour before we leave, so get moving."

James walked over and clasped a hand on Max's shoulder. "Thanks a lot for this. I really appreciate it."

"No problem, happy to help out." Max tipped his head toward me and I smiled.

The hatch door opened and James ushered me through. I stepped out into a small clearing in the center of some trees. Trees that looked exactly like the ones around our camp. I looked around. Nope, just more trees. It was the opposite of surprising.

James came up behind me and laughed. "I know what you're thinking. Be patient." He grabbed my hand. "This way, through those trees there."

The foliage was dense and thick but in less than twenty steps, we were out of it. I looked up and gasped. "The beach! It looks so different at night."

Now that we were out of the woods, I noticed the sky was lit up with stars, including the Weeping Boy. The two moons hung low like glowing orbs just above the horizon. And the sand took my breath away. It glowed a sparkling pink as though it was lit from underneath. The beach shimmered in iridescent color.

"Tell me that isn't the coolest thing you've seen," said James. "There was nothing close to this on Earth."

A light, warm breeze caressed my skin as I kicked off my shoes and wiggled my toes in the shimmering soft sand. Specks of pink glowed across the tops of my toes.

James tugged at my arm. "C'mon, I didn't just bring you here to look at it." He pulled me down to the water's edge. "We're going in."

My heart pounded in my chest. The thing I'd dreamed of doing forever—swimming in real water—was about to happen with James. I stared out into the abyss of ocean.

The water sparkled from the moonlight as the waves undulated across the surface. The warm water lapped over my feet, and I inhaled a deep breath of the fresh air. I was in real water and still couldn't get over that I could breathe whenever and wherever I wanted, without the use of any suits or contraptions.

A large wave crashed onto the shore and soaked my pants from the knees down. "Uh, I didn't exactly bring a swimsuit," I said.

A mischievous look came over James' face. "I didn't say you needed one." With that, he peeled his own shirt over his head and threw it into the sand. I tried not to stare but the moonlight highlighted his abs. God, he was gorgeous.

He took a step toward me and playfully tugged the bottom of my shirt, er, his shirt. "It's not like I haven't seen you before."

I gulped, remembering when I'd woken up in nothing but bandages and a medical gown. His lips brushed mine and the butterflies in my stomach kicked in. I stepped back and pulled the shirt over my head before tossing it next to his. This was my chance to figure out how to swim, and we only had an hour, so I had to make it count.

James took out his gun and dropped it in the sand, then yanked his pants down and stepped out of them. My jaw dropped. He looked downright hot standing there in nothing but underwear. He grinned, then turned and raced into the water. "Come catch me," he said and dove under the surface.

This was actually happening. I hesitated and looked around but the beach was deserted. Oh, what the hell. I pulled the gun from my waistband and put it with James' before slipping my pants down over my hips. After a deep breath, I dropped them all the way to my feet. All that remained were my thermoplastic panties. Though I dreaded getting them wet, there was no way I was taking them off. I waded into the water and made it waist deep before James surfaced again. He stood about ten feet away from me and ran his hand through his hair. I was all too aware that the moonlight didn't hide the fact that I was half naked. His eyes traveled down my body and back to my face.

"You're beautiful," he said. "Come here."

I took another step and shivered.

He moved through the water toward me. "Are you cold?"

I shook my head and undid my braid so that my hair fell around my shoulders. "No." It was true. The water was warm. It was the intensity of his stare that made my body react.

We met in the water and all I could think about was him kissing me again. Instead, he came around behind me and put his hand on my waist. "Are you ready?"

Yeah, I'd never been more ready. I leaned back into his body. "For what?"

He laughed and caressed my side. "To swim. Isn't that your dream?"

My body tingled at his touch. I wanted to swim, and we only had an hour. "Sure."

He pulled one of my arms back a little and then swept it over my head before doing the same with my other arm. He murmured into my ear. "This is how people used to swim on Earth when there was water, except you'd be horizontal." His hand trailed down my arm and lingered at my lower back.

I wished I could see his face. I turned to face him. "So far your swimming lesson seems as unorthodox as that medical exam back in my room in the bunker."

James laughed again. It was such a rare sound from him. I'd never seen him like this before and it made him even sexier. I leaned toward his lips. He kissed me briefly then pulled away. "After you learn how to swim. We live near water now and you should know how to do it."

It was the first time ever I'd wished he was more like Markus. "You've never been swimming before, Mr. Expert, so how do you know how to do it?" I challenged.

"I don't, I only saw an old video on the Net. This is my first time too," he said. "You can watch me make a fool of myself first."

I smiled. "Twist my arm."

He dove under again but rose to the surface and moved his arms in the way that he'd moved mine. It wasn't graceful, but it got the job done because he moved a few feet in the water before he came up coughing. "It's harder than it looks, but at least it's freshwater," he said when he caught his breath. "Oceans on Earth had salt in them."

I tried to ignore the water dripping off his body and scooped up a handful of water. "Mmm. Just like Caelia Pure."

He laughed. "Okay, enough stalling. Now you try."

I cringed. It would be just my luck that I'd die trying to learn to swim.

"Fine. Here goes." I put one arm in the air as I glided forward onto my stomach. Water went up my nose and I sputtered back upright again.

James eased up to my side. "Take it easy. I'm right here. Try again."

I wiped the water from my face. "Okay, I'll start out with what I did in the creek." I leaned back and floated, staring up at the dazzling sky. James stood next to me but I didn't dare look at him. I still wasn't over the fact that I was mostly naked.

His hand reached out to touch my stomach and I shivered again. One of his fingers lightly grazed the underside of my breast and heat spread through me like fire. If I didn't start swimming, I was pretty sure I was going to jump on him. I flipped over and moved my arms in the water. When I didn't get very far, I remembered that James had also kicked his legs.

After the need to breathe became apparent, I stood up and faced James. He was a good ten feet away. I fist pumped in the air. "I did it!"

James gave me a thumbs-up sign. "I'm impressed. Now swim back to me."

He didn't need to tell me twice. I dove under and pumped my legs as I rotated my arms. When I rose out of the water and smoothed my hair back, I didn't see James.

"You overshot me," he said and laughed from behind.

I couldn't believe I'd just swam in the ocean—it felt incredible. Something I'd dreamed of for years but never thought would happen. I turned to face James and walked to him. My nakedness was bothering me less and less under the intensity of his stare. I still felt vulnerable, but there was something liberating about allowing myself to be exposed to him. It felt natural. He took my hands in his.

His eyes drilled into mine under the light of the moon. I was nervous but we didn't have much time left. "So I swam like you wanted me to."

"And?" He reached out his hand toward me.

I smiled. "It was amazing, but I'm just wondering if we're done?"

James grasped my hips and pulled me to him in the waist-deep water until our chests touched. "No," he said. His voice sounded huskier. "We're not even close to done."

He leaned down and kissed my shoulder with feathery light kisses and moved slowly up my neck until he reached my mouth. I parted my lips and he kissed me slowly while he caressed my lower back with his hand. His kiss intensified and we slowly stepped toward the glowing shoreline as our mouths moved with greater urgency.

My hands traveled up and down his body as I explored every inch of him. My fingers traced the areas on his arms where he'd been shot by the Consulate, and then I touched the scar I'd seen on his lower back when we were in the bunker. I pulled back. "Where did you get this?" I asked breathlessly.

He nuzzled my neck and murmured into my ear. "It's the sign of the Resistance. Kale marked all of his soldiers. Britta had it too." His hands were all over me again. "Any more questions?"

I groaned. "No, I'm good for now."

We reached the shoreline and James eased me down onto the pillow-soft sand. I pulled him to me and brought his mouth to mine. Our bodies tangled together. His hands. My hands. The last bits of clothing coming off. Overwhelming sensations vibrated through me. Only the occasional lapping of gentle waves against my legs grounded me to reality. I forgot about everything else. There was no Consulate, no Kale, no dead mother or sister.

There was only James.

Chapter FOURTEEN

AS WE HEADED BACK TO CAMP IN MAX'S SHIP, I HAD THE BRIEF selfish thought to tell Max to keep going, to take us somewhere where James and I could be safe together. My head rested on James' shoulder as I sat in his lap. Max had taken one look at us and hadn't mentioned a word about flight safety. My clothes were damp, and I had sand in places I didn't know was possible, but I didn't care. It was the messiest I'd been in my whole carefully controlled life, and I'd never been happier.

James stroked my hair. "Is it bad that I don't want to go back?" he asked.

I sighed. "You stole my thoughts."

He kissed my neck. "It will all be fine. We'll do what we planned and then get out."

James sounded so sure, but doubt nagged at me. What if something went wrong? I nuzzled closer into him. His arms were strong and I felt safe there. Like nothing could hurt me, and it all could turn out okay. "Tell me about our first escape attempt that I don't remember."

"Let's see. Alec knew Dr. Sorokin's routine and snuck me into your room between rounds. When I first asked you to escape with me, you slapped me. I deserved it, by the way. It took a lot of talking, convincing, and explaining before you finally agreed." He chuckled. "Took even longer before you let me kiss you."

"I kissed you? Back in the containment center?" *Those dreams had been real.*

James leaned into my ear. "A few times, but you held back, until the day we ran. Right before we got caught, you kissed me like you meant it. It gave me hope."

A heat spread through me as I recalled that kiss. The one I'd thought was just an amazing dream.

James ran his hand up my arm. "That's why I was so confused when you came into the bar that day when I was talking with Sonya. I thought we were okay."

I shook my head. "I can't believe how powerful those drugs were. Even though I can remember everything now from before the containment center, my time there is still like a thick fog." I traced circles on his arm with my finger. "I'm still trying to come to terms with everything."

I thought of all that the Consulate had done to me, to James, to Dad, to the countless other victims they'd amassed. Maybe taking them down wouldn't be the worst thing. Maybe Kale was right. As we flew over the night-blanketed landscape, a question still nagged at me. "James, I have to ask. Do you still plan to get revenge on Allan Davis and the others who killed your family?"

He squeezed my hand. "Yeah, I still plan to get even. But I won't compromise your safety again now that I have you safe."

I looked into those hazel eyes of his. "I think Autumn and Callie would have loved this place. They wouldn't know what to do with all these flowers and leaves."

James smiled and squeezed my hand. "Yeah, they'd think Caelia was pretty kick-ass."

Markus, Lucy, and Alec were all asleep when we got back. The sky had a few tinges of gray, so we didn't have long to rest. James and I crept into Markus' hut and curled up together on the extra cot. I'd wanted to go to James' hut, but he worried that if we stayed away any longer, Alec would send out a search party to find me. Plus, we didn't have much time before we had to get moving. James and I lay facing each other and stared into each other's eyes. "Can I ask you something?" I whispered.

"Shoot," he said, then winced. "Sorry, bad choice of words."

"The thing about us both being able to fire my dad's guns? I don't get it. It's so rare for two people to have the same exact vibration."

James didn't say anything for a minute. "I'm not sure, but have you ever wondered . . . Never mind, it's cheesy."

"No, what?" I prompted.

James laced his fingers through mine. "Do you believe in soul mates?"

I stiffened. With everything we were facing, I didn't think I could handle where this conversation was going. "Maybe, why?"

"It's just that . . . I've read a lot on the Net, watched videos, though I'm sure not as many as you have. Even back when there were tons of people of Earth, it was rare to hear people say they found their soul mate. But once in a while, you'd hear a story. Like they were meant to be together."

I shifted, feeling uncomfortable. Yet I kept my hand in his. There wasn't room for love in a world like this, was there? Love had only ever brought me pain. Love ended in death. That's what my head said. I wasn't sure my heart was listening. "Are you saying you think that two people who are true soul mates have the same vibration?"

"Maybe," James said. "Something to think about anyway." He leaned over and kissed me gently on the lips. "Now, get some rest." As soon as he put his arm around me, I fell asleep.

"Wake up, sleepyhead." Markus shook my arm. "Time to get stuff done. Big day ahead."

I sat up and rubbed my eyes. James was gone. As I'd drifted off, I remembered he'd said that he was going to take care of Dad, but would be back.

Markus took one look at me and laughed. "I don't even want to know the reason your hair looks like that."

"What?" I fingered my sand-filled hair, which had dried as I slept and stuck out in weird angles. "Oh." I thought of the last few hours with James and blushed. "Um, I'll meet you outside."

A sunny, warm day greeted me. It was hard to shake the term "day" after using it for so many years. Plus a "sunny, warm light break" sounded weird. I dashed down to the creek and dunked my head under the cool water until I could get my fingers through it. It might be my last chance to bathe for a while.

Alec was outside wrestling around with Lucy when I returned to the camp. I was glad to see him having some fun for once.

Alec threw a stick and Lucy took off after it. "Did you have a fun time?" he asked.

I met his eyes. "I really did."

Alec sighed. "*Bueno.* I want you to be happy."

I smiled. "I want you to be happy too. Reed seems pretty cool, huh?"

Alec grinned.

James came racing back through the woods into the clearing.

"How is he?" I asked before James could catch his breath.

"Better," he said. "Still weak, but we'll get the guns, get him on the ship, and move out."

Markus emerged from the hut. "We ready to do this?" he asked. "Also, what exactly are we doing?"

James steadied his shoulders and adjusted the pack on his back. "We're as ready as we're gonna be. *I'm* going to town to see if I can get Sonya to tell me where the weapons are, but we need a backup plan if she won't. Markus, I thought you could do flyovers of the area. Maybe you'll see something from the air."

"I can go with Markus," said Alec. "He could use an extra pair of eyes to make sure we don't miss anything."

James nodded. "That's what I was going to suggest. Bring Lucy with you. If everything goes as planned, we'll take off as soon as we get the guns and Tora's dad."

I was going with James. My satchel was packed with Callie's picture, and I'd stuffed the page with the gun formulas in there too, though I still didn't know what I was going to do with it.

Markus slung his pack over his shoulder. "Got it. We'll keep you posted through the com system."

"I'm counting on you, Markus."

He grinned. "And I'm counting on you to find a cute *señorita* or two to bring along. Preferably three."

"Be careful, you two," Alec said, though he looked at me. He grabbed his things and called out to Lucy. "Do you want to go for a ride in a ship?" he asked her. "Do you, girl?"

Lucy wagged her tail like it was the best idea she'd ever heard.

"Come on, then, Lucy," Markus said. "We don't have all day."

She bounded over, her tail wagging at warp speed.

Markus laughed. "I've never had a female run that fast to me before." He turned to leave, then walked back and hugged me.

I gave him an awkward pat on the back. "What's that for?" I asked.

"Don't know," he said. "Just don't die, okay?"

"I'll do my best."

Markus stared at me a second longer and nodded. "Good." He looked at Alec. "Let's motor, we got work to do."

They headed farther into the woods, past our camp, toward the area where Markus remembered parking his ship. I hoped they found it quickly.

James and I headed in the opposite direction, back along the creek toward the bar. We'd discussed this part of the plan while flying back from the beach on Max's ship. Originally, James didn't think it was safe for us to separate and wanted me to come with him to see Sonya. I figured she'd be more likely to give him information without me there. He'd already used his com device to set up a meeting at the command center.

While James was talking to Sonya at the bar, I'd meet with a small group at the center. That way, Sonya wouldn't be able to report our plan back to Kale if she wasn't really on our side. James had only invited to the meeting those Resistance members that he thought would be open to leaving with us. We'd have them help move Dad once the guns were loaded on Markus' ship.

Anxiety knotted my stomach. It didn't seem so simple now that we were doing it. I tried to think about all the things that could go wrong—which pretty much involved everything.

If Sonya had been swayed by Kale's bravado and grand plans regarding a Consulate takedown, I doubted she would be an open book about the location of the guns. Yet, she'd bragged about seeing the weapons and had tried to tell James something important the night before, so maybe there was hope.

I was also consumed by guilt. Guilt that the people we were forced to leave behind would be defenseless against the Consulate. Their measly guns wouldn't stand a chance against Consulate ships. Dad's guns could help them, but it was too dangerous for us to stay with them. At least that's what I'd told myself.

The wildflowers were in full bloom and their scent wafted through the trees as we walked toward the center. As beautiful as they smelled, they sent pangs of pain through my heart. If everything went according to plan, I had no idea how long it would be before I could smell real flowers again.

"Hold up a second," James said. I hadn't noticed that he'd plucked one of the flowers. He tucked it behind my ear and smiled. "Alec can find someone else to give flowers to. That's for good luck. Now Callie will be with you."

I wiped a tear away. "Thanks. That means a lot."

He gave me a brief, tender kiss on the lips. "I still think about Autumn a lot and know how much it hurts. We'll get through this."

I touched his cheek. "I hope so."

We hurried toward the bar and stopped when we reached the clearing. "Be careful," I said. "I don't have a com device, so you better get your ass to the command center soon. Don't make me worry."

James gave me a quick kiss. "I'll be right there. What could possibly go wrong?"

I groaned. "You can't say that. It's like tempting fate."

He smiled. "You never struck me as someone who believed in fate. Now get going. See you soon."

It took so much effort to get my feet to move away from him. "See you soon." He jogged toward the bar and I watched him before I headed toward the command center. It had grown so warm that I sweated in my light T-shirt and pants. It was nothing compared to the blistering inferno back on Earth, but I couldn't help my momentary flicker of fear. I glimpsed the yellow sun through the trees and relaxed. We'd have billions of years before we had to worry about that again.

The command center looked deserted when I approached. No guards stood outside. I knew James had relayed the plan to Max on the com system, but wondered if Max had gotten the word out fast enough. The windows and door were shut tight. I crept up to the door and pulled.

It opened easily and I peeked inside. Everything was dark.

"Tora!"

I jumped a foot in the air as I scrambled for my gun.

"Sshhh." A hand grabbed my arm and pulled me inside. "It's just me, Reed. James said this should be top secret."

My heart raced. "It just would have been helpful if I'd known *how* top secret ahead of time."

I looked around at some faces that I recognized, like Edgar, Trent, and Ian. There were others that I didn't know, including a few girls. Markus would be thrilled.

Edgar came to stand at my side and started speaking Spanish to the group. I held up my hand. "You lost me at *hola*. I think we're good as far as the secret thing, so can we please talk in English?"

"*Sí, lo siento,*" Edgar said. He cleared his throat and addressed the room. "We are gathered here to discuss a plan to move to a new location. If Kale is to be believed, the Consulate is close to finding us and plans to wipe us out as soon as possible. We could stay and fight, but then Kale would maintain control of the weapons, and some members of the Resistance—myself included—believe that he has lost his way."

"So what does that make us?" one man asked. "The Resistance against the Resistance? We're just going to give up everything we've been fighting for?"

"No, Connor," said Trent. "We're still resisting the Consulate, but Kale's methods have become too similar to theirs. I don't consider Kale the leader of the Resistance anymore. That title goes to James, in my opinion." Trent looked to me. "No disrespect meant to your dad, of course, but I don't think he's interested in leading a revolution anymore."

He was right about that.

"Yes," agreed Reed. "James."

I sucked in my breath. Though I agreed that James was the best person for the job, I had some idea what that job description entailed, and I didn't like it. Being named the leader of the Resistance meant you might as well paint a huge target on yourself. The Consulate would know exactly who to kill first.

"I'm not sure we need to get all formal with titles," I said, but no one was listening to me. Their eyes were on Edgar. He certainly had a commanding presence.

"We are the hope for a new world," he said. "There are small groups on nearby moons and planets. Imagine how we could help them if we join forces. When the Consulate attacks here, they'll only find power-hungry people like Kale left. It will be violence and greed against the same, and we will remain safe away from the bloodshed. Upon our return, we will form a land of peace and harmony."

It sounded great in theory, yet I still doubted whether such a small group could manage to carry it off.

Edgar bowed to me. "Tora, we are at your service. Just tell us what you need and we'll help." He straightened and addressed the group. "I'm going to say this one more time. It is imperative that no one speaks of this plan outside this group. As we all know, there are those whose sympathies shift with the changing of the winds." Edgar turned back to me. "I assure you, we are not those people."

All eyes fell on me. I was glad I'd taken the time to wash the crazy angles out of my hair. "Basically, we need any info at all on where the guns might be. Some people are looking, and James is talking to Sonya as we speak."

"I'm sure Sonya wishes they were doing more than talking," said Connor.

Someone snickered across the room.

"That ain't gonna happen," said Reed, clutching my arm protectively. "But Sonya did say that she saw the guns, so hopefully we'll know something soon."

"Oh," said a girl who introduced herself as Becca, probably the same Becca that Markus had mentioned earlier. "I didn't hear anything about the guns, but Sonya mentioned that Kale took her somewhere *romantic*."

Sonya had been talking about her ideal man. Hard to imagine that person was Kale . . .

"Anyone else have any ideas about where the guns might be?"

"No," Ian said. "I saw Sonya and Kale head toward his ship the other day, but I didn't know where he was taking her."

That wasn't a lot to go on. I really hoped that James was getting information out of her.

"We'll see what James finds out," I said. "And then we need to get my dad. Any ideas on where to relocate?"

Edgar scratched his chin. "There's a nearby planet, Dais, with a small colony. I know there's water, but it's all underground and a bitch to get to. Heard it's mostly rocks and dirt. Don't know much else, but that might be our best bet." He turned to the group. "Collect supplies and pack everything that we'll need quickly, but don't arouse suspicion. Kale's men can't know what we're doing. Go now and only use the com system if you need to. Switch to channel twenty-one, but know that it's possible Kale and his men could catch something on there. We'll meet back here when the clock strikes the next groove."

James still hadn't arrived, and I kept watching the door. The plan was already off track. Edgar sat down on one of the benches after everyone else had left. He pulled out his com device and set it on the bench next to him. "I'll wait here until James gets back. Why don't you go visit with your dad?"

I didn't want to leave without seeing James, but I really wanted to see Dad. He was all alone out there in the woods.

Edgar must have sensed my hesitation. "I'll tell James where you are. We'll come to help move your dad as soon as James gets here. I promise. You won't be able to support your dad on your own, anyway."

"Thanks, Edgar." I opened the door and wished I'd see James running toward me through the clearing. No such luck.

I ran into the woods, even though, in the back of my mind, I knew I should have waited.

Chapter FIFTEEN

I TRIED TO REMEMBER THE WAY TO DAD'S HUT. THE TREES were thick and I didn't want to get lost. We would get Dad out of here, far away from Kale's reach.

I walked about as far as I thought I'd gone last time, then stopped and listened. A few birds sang up ahead and every once in a while a breeze blew through the trees. The hut had to be close.

"Dad?" I whispered. I really hoped Kale would be gone as long as James had thought. Still, we didn't have a ton of time.

Another of the brightly colored winged insects darted in front of me. It flew upward and then glided down before zipping behind a tree. I walked after it to get a glimpse of its breathtaking aerial dynamics. Just beyond the tree was Dad's hut. I forgot about the insect and raced to the door. *Please let him be okay.*

I peeled back the flap and hurried inside. Dad was sitting up on the cot. It was the first time I'd seen him upright. "Dad!" I ran to hug him. "How are you feeling?"

"I'm doing a little better. Must be that medicine that James gave me." He squeezed my hand. "That's a good kid, that James."

I smiled. "Yeah. Most of the time, anyway. We're going to get you out of here. Markus is going to fly us somewhere safe."

Dad chuckled. "So, Markus pulled through for us. I wasn't sure how he would turn out. He always struck me as more opportunist than activist."

Opportunist was the perfect word for Markus. "He's been through a lot and has had some bumps in the road lately," I said, "but I definitely like him more than I did back on Earth."

"Good." Dad patted my arm. "When do we get out of here? Is Kale helping us?" Dad tried to stand up but wobbled on his feet. I put my arm around him to steady him.

"Take it easy, Dad. I don't trust Kale, and some of the others don't either. James is leading us now. He should be here any minute and he'll help get you to the ship once the guns are on board." I helped him take a step. "Since you've been the leader all this time, it would be great if you put your support behind James."

Dad's eyes widened. "I'm not sure what's going on, Tora, but Kale saved my life. We should talk this through with him."

I sighed. "Dad, he saved you because he wants the formulas. The ones you gave the Consulate. He took your guns from me by force. He'll do anything to get what he wants. That's why we have to leave now."

Dad groaned as he took a tentative step. He was much thinner than he used to be which made it easier to support his weight. "Those guns. My biggest regret is making them. They've brought nothing but devastation and death."

We made it to the tent flap, and I helped him get outside. "I know, Dad. But we're going to get rid of them before they can cause more damage. Once the guns are gone, it won't matter if someone can rekey them. C'mon, we gotta keep moving."

Dad took weak, shuffling steps. I just wanted to get deeper into the trees so we had some more cover. "How strong you are to have survived everything you went through with losing Callie, Mom, your home . . ." His voice broke.

I shook my head. "No, you're the strong one to have been held captive for so long. We've both made it through and we have all the time in the world to catch up. I'm not going anywhere. But now we have to be quiet."

Voices drifted through the woods.

"See," I said. "James and his friends are coming as we speak—"

My heart stopped when I realized the voice didn't belong to James. It was Kale. And it sounded like he had several of his soldiers with him. Dad would never be able to outrun them in his condition, and I wasn't leaving without him.

I pulled Dad into a group of shrubs. A bug buzzed in my ear, and I tried to swat it away with the hand that wasn't supporting Dad. Sweat dripped into my eyes and my heart hammered in my chest. I reached into my waistband and pulled out my gun.

"Tora, is this necessary?" Dad whispered. "I'm sure Kale will listen to reason."

I shook my head. Reason wasn't Kale's strong suit. Killing was. Britta would attest to that if she could.

"Well, isn't this fine and dandy?" Kale's voice echoed loudly through the woods. "Looks like Mr. Reynolds has made a getaway, and he sure as hell didn't do it on his own. Spread out and find them. Now!" Footsteps pounded past us as Kale's men fanned out. We were lucky they'd assumed we'd made it farther than twenty feet beyond the hut.

Kale's voice faded as he moved away through the trees. I waited until there was only silence. Dad and I had to move, but I had no idea which way led to safety, and which would lead us right to Kale and his men.

Dad leaned into me and I realized he'd used up most of his strength already. I wished I had a com device and could call for help.

"Can you go a little farther?" I asked Dad, helping him to his feet.

His face was pale. "I'll try. I don't understand. I've never heard Kale so angry before."

"I think anger has consumed him," I said in a hushed voice. "He's driven by it. I think he thinks it makes him stronger."

We moved toward the back of the command center. Maybe Edgar would still be there. Every sound seemed like a potential threat and every time I thought I heard heavy breathing, I realized it was my own.

Dad was getting harder to support, and I didn't know how long he could keep going. A branch snapped nearby and I tried to lift my gun and keep Dad standing at the same time.

"Oh, thank god!" James grabbed hold of Dad's other arm.

I sighed in relief. "You have no idea how glad I am to see you."

James called a cryptic message into his com system. A minute later, Edgar appeared.

"It would have been helpful to have one of those, you know?"

Edgar took over the arm that I'd been holding. James and Edgar wrapped Dad's arms around their necks and carried him like he was a twig.

"I didn't think you'd need it," James said. "Kale wasn't supposed to be back yet."

"What did Sonya tell you?" I asked.

"Nothing," James said. "She didn't show up."

"What? Why?" That seemed strange, even for her.

"I don't know," he admitted.

"But that, combined with Kale showing up early, is awfully coincidental," Edgar said.

A voice came through the com system and James put it to his ear. "Okay, Kale's men have been spotted north and west of here. We'll head to a hut encampment farther east and have Markus land his ship and pick us up there."

"And the guns?" I asked.

"Not sure yet. Let's get you guys safe first and then figure that out."

We passed the back of the bar and command center and continued moving.

I kept my weapon powered up. A part of me wondered if I'd ever be able to live without having to be armed at all times.

"James," Dad said, breathing heavily, "Tora tells me that you are leading the Resistance now."

"Well, sir, I'm leading a group of people who want me to lead them. Kale still has his followers though."

Dad sighed. "Being a leader is a great responsibility. It took over my life and . . . my relationships suffered greatly for it."

I remembered all the hours Dad had spent in his study, doing what I thought was Consulate work, while Mom disappeared further and further into herself and her pain meds. But James wasn't Dad, and I sure as hell wasn't my mom.

"I know, sir. I just want people to be able to live the life they choose. Not everyone wants Kale's way. I'm just trying to help people."

"That's how I started out too. I hope you can succeed where I failed. Not sure if I really ended up helping anyone in the end."

"I'm still alive and kicking," I said. "So you helped me."

"And James is a natural leader," Edgar added. "He doesn't have the ego that Kale does. He'll lead us into a new peaceful future."

That sounded lovely. I just wished it would happen.

We reached a group of huts that looked abandoned. The fire pit was untouched. "Perfect," Dad said. "I'm spent."

Edgar and James carried him inside and I followed. The cots looked like they'd never been used. "Whose huts are these?" I asked.

"They were built for some of the guests from other colonies. Some people come to check us out. Some stay, others leave," Edgar explained.

Dad lay on the cot and settled his head back against the thin bedding. "I'm feeling a little better, but just need to rest a minute."

"Of course, Dad." I pulled the cover over his legs, then sat next to him, and looked up at James. "What now?"

"There's a clearing not far from here. I'll call Max and go out there to flag him down. He'll be closer than Markus. It should only take a few minutes. Edgar, can you get back to the command center and contact the others? If Sonya told Kale what she knows about our plans, then he knows about me, but not you. You should be safe if you run into any of his men."

"Yes, sir. We'll wait for your next orders but I'll get everyone together." Edgar saluted and headed back out.

James came over and gave Dad another vial of meds. "This should help with the fatigue and keep you going until we're out of here. Tora, why don't you come with me to get Max?"

I shook my head. "I'm not leaving Dad. I'll wait with him. It'll only be a few minutes, right?"

James sighed. "I thought you'd say that. Ten, fifteen minutes tops. Please stay safe for that long." He touched my hand and stared into my eyes.

Dad pushed himself up to a sitting position with sudden determination. "James, can I tell you something?" he asked.

James tore his eyes away from mine. His face was serious as he addressed my dad. "Yes, sir."

Dad looked somehow stronger than he had a minute earlier. His eyes even held a hint of the calm confidence he'd had back on Earth in the bunker. He stared at James. "I want to be crystal clear. There will never, ever be peace as long as my weapons exist. You must find a way to get rid of them once and for all."

I recognized the conflict that crossed James' face because I felt it too. Nothing would make me happier than getting rid of those burner guns, but I couldn't shake the feeling that we might need them first.

James and I exchanged glances.

"It's a slippery slope," Dad said. "Once you start justify-ing some actions, it gets easier to justify others. Believe me, I know. One day you wake up and aren't so sure if maybe you're not the bad guy after all."

"You're right," James said, nodding. "It's a line that I plan to stay on the right side of." James grasped my fingers with his and I watched Dad's gaze fall to our hands.

"I better get going." James leaned over and gave me a quick kiss on the lips before dashing out of the hut.

"Ah, young love," Dad said, smiling. "I remember those days. So many things I should have done differently. Don't make my same mistakes. Love is more important than anything else."

He started to lie back down but then gripped my wrist. "I wasn't kidding, you know."

"About what, Dad?"

"Love. I know it sounds ridiculous to say, with the cir-cumstances being what they are, but it's true. As long as those guns are around, love will never win." His grip loos-ened.

"I know, Dad, I know." Part of me thought he was right, and part of me thought that he didn't fully understand the situation. He sat up and swung his legs over the side of the cot. "You know what, I'm feeling better every minute. I'll help James in any way that I can."

I laughed. He seemed more and more like the Dad I'd grown up with. "Okay, but let's just wait a few minutes. You want to get your strength up."

We sat side by side and listened to the sounds outside as we talked about life in the pod city. A trilling birdcall was interrupted by voices yelling. I jumped up in anticipation. That was even faster than James had thought it would take. He'd only been gone a few minutes.

The voices grew closer and my blood turned to ice when I realized one of them was Kale's. We'd seriously underestimated his tracking skills. My hand closed on my gun. I had no idea how many there were, and wasn't sure I could get them all in time.

Dad gestured at the cot. "Get under," he whispered. "The blankets will hide you. Give me your gun."

I paused a second and shoved my gun into his hand. "Okay, but don't trust him. Don't tell him anything. Keep this under the covers and don't hesitate to use it if he threatens you." I scrambled under the bed as Dad lay down and covered himself with the blankets. The edges hung over the side, and I tugged at them until they nearly touched the floor. I backed up until I was against the wall and curled up to make myself as small as possible.

Kale's voice boomed outside of the hut. "Vlad Tepes! I'm tired of this crap. Wait here and don't let anyone come close. I won't be long."

"Yes, sir," several voices answered in response. *How many were there?*

I heard the flap of the hut move aside. "Howdy, Micah," said Kale. "How are we feeling? I trust that the meds James gave you must have had some impact since you've been able to move to a more scenic location, and all." His boots scraped against the floor as he came over to Dad. "I mean, the trees are so much greener over here. I'm sure it was well worth the hike."

Dad coughed. "Yes, much better. Just tired."

The cot creaked as Kale sat on the edge of the bed. I could see his shoes through the small sliver of space between the covers and the floor. If I wanted, I could reach out and touch him. My heart hammered in my chest and my throat constricted in fear. Why had I given Dad the gun? I felt naked and completely useless without my weapon. If I had it, I could shoot Kale in the leg right now and finish him before the soldiers made it into the tent. I wasn't sure what would happen after that, but at least we'd have a chance.

Maybe Kale just wanted information from Dad and then he would leave.

"Excellent," said Kale. "I'm glad you're better because I really need some help."

Dad coughed loudly again. "With what?"

I hoped he wasn't coughing to cover up any sound I was making. It felt like my heartbeat was so loud that it echoed in the hut.

"We all appreciate your dedication and service to the Resistance. Word has come that the Consulate is planning a devastating attack on us to wipe us out for good. I'm sure you're aware that your daughter is in the area? Has she been by to visit you yet? You want to keep her safe from those Consulate burners, don't you?"

"Yes," Dad said. "I've heard she's alive, thank goodness, and I hope to see her very soon." He coughed again. "But I don't understand how I can help you in a Consulate battle. I'm afraid I'm not in fighting shape at the moment."

Kale sighed. "Your weapons, Micah. They are the only thing that can possibly defeat the Consulate ships. We have them in our possession, but it seems that no one I trust can fire them. That the trigger keys have some sort of code that is preventing us from using them."

Dad shifted in the bed. "And how did you come about getting my guns, anyway?"

A moment of silence. Why was he going there? I wanted to tell him to stop talking. He probably didn't know it, but he was making it worse.

Kale chose his words carefully. "Tora gave them to me, of course. She really believes in this fight and said she would do anything to help her father's work continue."

"Really?" Dad asked. "That doesn't sound like my Tora at all."

Don't, Dad. Don't do this.

The cot creaked and it sounded like Dad was trying to sit up. Good, maybe he was situating himself so he could shoot Kale with my gun. "In fact, my daughter believed that the guns should be destroyed. I'd be very surprised if she gave the weapons to you willingly." Dad cleared his throat and continued. "Do you see how far you've strayed from our mission, Kale? We wanted nothing but to be allowed to live in peace away from the Consulate."

No! This was not part of the plan. He had to be pissing off Kale big-time.

Kale stood up and took several steps away from the bed. He turned and faced Dad, who was fully upright and had swung his feet over the side of the cot. My stomach twisted inside and I clenched my fists. *Shoot him. Shoot him now.*

"So naive," Kale said. "How does one live in peace without weapons to protect oneself? Those Consulate burners need to be taught a lesson, and I'm going to be the one to take them down for what they did to innocent people."

"You are governed by anger, not reason," Dad said. "When your primary motivation changes from justice to revenge, no good can come of it."

Kale clucked his tongue. "I don't need your philosophical rubbish, old man. You only have one use right now, the one reason why I risked my ass to save you from the Consulate. I need those trigger formulas and I need them now."

"And if I say no?" Dad asked. He'd stopped coughing.

"Then that leaves zero uses for you." Kale took one more step back. "So what's it gonna be? We could be a great team, you and me. Leading a Resistance so powerful that no one could touch us."

"The world doesn't need more power. It needs more peace." Dad's voice sounded so tired.

I heard the sound of a gun powering up, and it wasn't mine. Sweat dripped from my hairline into my eyes. Why wasn't Dad shooting him? What was the point of asking for my gun if he hadn't intended to use it?

"Last chance," Kale said. "And to be clear, there's only one right answer here."

Dad spoke slowly. "I'm afraid I can't help you, Kale. I wish you could see how similar you've become to your enemy. The killing of innocent people was supposedly one of the reasons you despised the Consulate."

The cot was very still. Dad didn't seem like he was even trying to reach for his gun. I wanted to fly out from under the bed and claw Kale's eyes out with my bare hands.

"If you're not with us, then you're against us," Kale replied calmly. "That doesn't make you innocent; it makes you the enemy. And you know I can't abide enemies."

A laser fired and Dad's body fell off the bed to the floor. A scream rose in my throat but I stifled it. Kale's heavy footsteps walked to the hut entrance and he left. I heard him call out to the others. "Well that was a big, ole waste of my time. Looks like we're going to have to make James help us after all. Let's go find him."

They retreated into the woods, talking loudly as they went. I crawled out from under the cot and rushed to Dad's side. Blood pooled underneath him. He had a laser blast through his abdomen. His eyes were slitted.

Tears streamed down my face. I pressed my T-shirt onto the wound but the blood soaked right through it. The hole in his stomach was too large. I held his hand. "Hold on, Dad, I'll get James."

Dad's voice was barely more than whisper. "Don't think even James can fix this."

I couldn't stop crying. "Why? Why didn't you shoot him when you had the chance?"

"The others . . . would have . . . killed you. Couldn't risk that." His eyes weren't focusing. "I want you . . ." His breathing became ragged. ". . . to live . . . a long, happy life. Live for . . . those of us . . . who can't." His eyes closed.

I flung myself over his body. "Don't go, Dad. I love you."

He exhaled one long, uneven breath and lay still. I sobbed and lay down on the floor next to him. It was such a cruel act of fate to have found him alive, only to have him ripped away from me again. Permanently. I wrapped my arm around him and turned on my side. I didn't care if Kale returned and found me. The plan didn't seem to matter with Dad dead. Dead because of all those guns. I hated those guns, but not nearly as much as I hated Kale. I'd heard what Dad told Kale about how no good can come of it when your motivation is based on revenge rather than justice.

That might be the case but I was going to get revenge anyway, and good would come out of it. Because Kale would be dead. My goals were simple and crystal clear. Get the guns. Kill Kale.

It was good to have goals.

Chapter SIXTEEN

FOOTSTEPS POUNDED THROUGH THE FOREST AS I LAY NEXT to Dad, my arm still wrapped around him. The gun. It was still under the covers on the cot. I scrambled to my feet, slipped on the blood-covered floor, and smashed back down onto my knees. James and Max tore into the tent, weapons raised.

"We heard gunfire—" Max said, before his eyes widened in horror. His gun fell to the floor.

James rushed to my dad and bent his head to listen to his chest. "He's gone."

"They're all gone now." My voice rose an octave.

Max stared at James. I'm sure I looked crazy. I was covered in Dad's blood—it was in my hair, on my clothes, my face.

I walked to the cot, retrieved my unused gun, and

tucked it into my waistband. "Soon Kale will be gone too. Then he can rot in hell for what he's done."

James came over and touched my arm. "Tora, I'm so sorry."

Fresh tears poured from my eyes. With plentiful water and adequate hydration I could apparently cry for an eternity. I swiped away tears with the back of my arm. "I want him to pay."

James smoothed my bloodied hair and tucked it behind my ear. "Yeah, I know what that feels like, but trust me, I'm not sure you want to go through with it."

"I didn't want to go through any of this." I crossed my arms. "And tell me that you don't still want to see Allan Davis dead."

James looked into my eyes. "I do want him dead, but not more than I want you alive. If I can only have one of those things, I want you." He pulled me toward him and encircled me in a tight hug.

A hug is exactly how Callie would have tried to make me feel better. I put my head on James' shoulder and cried. He didn't even seem to mind that I was getting blood all over him. I looked over his shoulder at Dad's body. He'd escaped confinement only to die at the hands of the same person who'd saved him. It wasn't fair. I imagined Callie waiting for him somewhere beyond this world and hoped he found her.

I raised my head from James' shoulder. "Can we move him somewhere better than this?"

"Yes, but for now it will have to be in the woods. Anywhere else and Kale will know about it."

Max agreed. "We can take him into the woods and come back when it's dark. The sky is already losing light."

"What about the meat monsters?" I said.

James called someone on the com device. "Some of the others are coming to help. We'll dig a shallow grave. It should keep the animals away until we can move him."

The idea of putting Dad in the ground sickened me, yet the thought of him being monster food was worse.

"Okay," I sniffed. But something bothered me. "Wait, who did you just call?"

James frowned. "Edgar, why?"

"Are you sure he's okay? I mean, why did Kale come back here so quickly, anyway?"

James clenched his jaw and Max answered. "That would be thanks to Sonya. She blew off her meeting with him. I asked her where she'd been and she said something like 'oh, now James needs me instead of his precious Tora' and that we'd all be sorry."

"She probably called Kale on his com channel to tell him about the meeting," James added. "I should have guessed it was a setup. Maybe I could have stopped this."

"I never heard Kale's ship," said Max. "He must have landed a ways out and traveled here by foot with his men."

Red-hot rage consumed me, and I added Sonya to the list of people I intended to kill. "I'm taking down that red-haired burner," I said. I tried to get a grip on my anger.

"Any word from Markus about the weapons?"

James shook his head. "He hasn't found anything. I'm going to tell him to head back, but be careful where he lands. Kale's men are probably on the hunt for all of us."

I told James and Max about Kale saying he'd need James now, since he couldn't rekey the triggers.

"He'll need me to do what he wants with your dad's guns, and then he'll kill me for being a traitor. The guy has lost it."

The others arrived a few minutes later, led by Edgar. I followed as they carried Dad's body deeper into the woods, far enough from the hut that we wouldn't be heard if Kale and his men returned. The others had brought shovels, but first they used their guns to laser the ground, to make it easier to dig.

"Do you want to leave?" James asked me, concern etched on his face. "I'm not sure you should see this."

"No, I'll stay. I need to see that Dad's at rest."

As James and the others dug away, I walked a short distance until I found some wildflowers and plucked a handful. The pink and white petals were a stark contrast to my blood-caked hand. I closed my eyes and inhaled the sweet scent. It brought me back to the dream I had of floating through the clouds and meeting Callie.

Find Dad, I pleaded silently. *You can all be together again.*

I squeezed my eyes shut as more tears threatened to leak out. Stupid tears. They were totally useless and couldn't bring Dad back, so I didn't see the point of them.

When I returned to the group, I noticed the grave was on the deeper side of shallow. They must have come to the same conclusion I had. They stared at the makeshift bouquet in my hands.

"Who am I kidding?" I asked. "We're not going to be able to come back here, maybe not ever."

James studied my face before digging the shovel deeper into the ground. The others silently copied the motion. Soon, they were ready to lift Dad's body into the ground. It had been different on Earth when all the bodies were disposed of by sun incineration. Even when someone had died inside the pod cities, they put them outside to burn. Put them out on the ground in the daylight, and they'd be dust by night.

I joined the others around Dad's grave. The sky had darkened and we didn't have much time. I knelt down and said a silent good-bye before dropping the flowers onto my father's chest. He'd have part of Callie to keep his body company, though I hoped the rest of him was elsewhere. I stood and nodded to the others, who started shoveling the dirt back into the hole. *I love you, Dad.* Tears flowed again, and this time I was ready to go. Instead of thinking of Dad in the ground, I wanted to remember the times I sat reading in his study while he worked in his notebooks at the desk.

I wiped more tears from my eyes. "We don't have the guns, we don't know where Kale and his men are, and the Consulate is supposedly about to attack. What do we do now?"

Max wiped the sweat from his face with his shirt. "We probably should figure out a new plan."

"We'll finish here," said Edgar to James. "Why don't you and Max take Tora to get cleaned up? Stick to the woods and away from the camps to avoid Kale's men."

"We'll see if Markus has found out anything about the guns and I'll be in touch before dark." James touched my arm, sweat dripping from his hair. "Let's get you to the creek."

I felt numb. Max walked just ahead to make sure it was safe. We traveled through the woods, careful to avoid the clearing by the bar. The winged insects and birds chattering and zipping around barely registered in my consciousness. We wound our way through the trees, overshooting the camps to make sure we were nowhere near Kale. By the time we reached the creek, the sun barely hovered on the horizon. Streaks of red and orange slashed through the sky. It looked like blood.

Max stood guard by a large tree while James dropped his pack along with my gun and accompanied me to the creek. I stepped into the water and walked to the center, submerging my arms while I watched the blood swirl away. My shirt was hopeless. The stains would never come out. I started crying again.

"Shhh," James murmured into my ear. "It's okay."

I scrubbed furiously at my hands, trying to clean the blood from under my nails. "No, it's not okay. This was your shirt."

"Huh?"

"I took it . . . back on Kale's ship. I wanted something of yours." I splashed my face and rubbed it until the water was clear. "There, I told you."

When I sat down and leaned my hair back into the water, James knelt next to me and wound his hands into it. He massaged the blood out in a gentle, rotating motion. "That's sweet," he said. "But don't worry. I have a few extra in my pack."

"Let me guess . . . they're white." I remembered the drawers that brimmed with nothing but white socks and shirts.

"Of course," he said. He paused. "Do you need more meds for your ankle?"

I sat up and wrung out my hair. "The pain is nothing compared to what I feel inside. Got anything for that?"

James took my hand and helped me up. "You know I do, but I'm guessing you don't really want it. This is one of those kinds of pains you want to keep."

I tried to manage a smile but couldn't. "You know me so well."

When we got to the tree, Max turned around while James dug a fresh T-shirt out of his pack and handed it to me. "Here you go. You'll have to deal with the pants for now. I don't have any extras and they'd fall off you, anyway."

"That's okay. These'll dry." I pulled off my shirt and tossed it onto the ground. It was almost completely crimson. I never wanted to see it again. The pants were a little less stained, though not by much. I yanked the clean shirt over my head and picked up my gun. "I guess I should hold this until my pants dry out." I didn't want to risk it getting wet and not working again.

I looked up at James. "Hey, you're wet too."

He shrugged. "No big deal. I'll be fine."

Grief got the better of me, and I put my arms around his neck. "Thank you. I'm not used to people taking care of me."

James kissed my forehead. "I know you can take care of yourself, but I hope you'll let me help out once in a while."

Max coughed. "Is it okay if I turn around now?"

"Oh, sorry, yes," I said. "Thanks for helping with all this."

He looked up at the darkening sky. "I'm happy to help, but we need to figure out where to go from here."

"Where will be safe from Kale?" I asked. "Do we sleep in the woods?"

"We need to find his ship before he takes off with the guns," said James.

I thought a minute. "Kale has a thing for flying at night. He thinks he's clever that way. I bet he'll leave and come back just before the light break. He doesn't want to get killed before he can regroup and figure out a new plan, and he can't do anything without someone to fire those guns."

James studied me. "Then we get everyone in our ships,

get some rest, and wait to see where Kale lands when he returns."

Max looked back and forth between us. "I hate to play devil's advocate, but how important are the guns? If we took off now, we could relocate everyone without worrying about Kale."

"The Consulate has people who can rekey them. And it's not like there are tons of other colonies where we can hide. Kale, or the Consulate, or someone else will figure out how to use the guns. With the weapons out there, no one will ever be able to live in peace. I have to finally get rid of them."

James raised an eyebrow.

"We, I mean."

Max sighed. "I guess you're right. Sometimes, I just wish the easy way out was the right way. Why doesn't it ever work that way?"

James pulled out his com and called Markus to find out his location. Unfortunately, Markus hadn't seen any sign of the weapons. James told him to move to an area near Max's ship, while Max called the others on his com. We'd meet up with them and split into two groups. We'd take shifts to search the skies for signs of Kale.

James, Max, and I trekked back through the woods. Exhaustion racked my body and I hoped the meeting place wasn't far away. Sad as it was, I actually missed living in the bunker at the moment. I could take a nap anytime I wanted, and since I'd been alone for years on end, it was a frequent occurrence. I'd even choose a nap over more beach time alone with James at the moment, which proved my insane sleep deprivation.

I took James' hand when he offered it and kept my gun in my free hand. At least I'd be prepared if we came across a meat monster. We walked in silence following Max.

After what must have been close to a mile, Max turned and whispered, "I think we're about there." He spoke into his com device.

The sound of another com device came from nearby. "We're here." Edgar's large form stepped out from behind a tree and motioned the others to follow him. It was difficult to make out who was who in the darkness. Thick clouds covered both moons and most of the stars. I spotted Reed's light hair in the group.

She ran up and hugged me. "I heard what happened to your dad. I'm so, so sorry."

I'd never been hugged so much in my life but I was getting more used to it. "Thanks."

"We're here too, sweetcakes. You okay?" I looked to my left, and Markus and Alec appeared at my side.

I threw my arms around Markus in a bear hug. "Markus, it's so good to see you." I was surprised that I meant it, and more surprised that I was turning into the hugger. Maybe it was contagious.

Alec touched my arm and gave me a gentle squeeze.

"What's the plan?" Edgar asked.

James gave him a brief rundown. "Any questions?"

"No, sir," said Edgar. "We should split into two groups."

Reed linked her arm through mine. "I'm going with Tora." She was so sweet—she couldn't have been more the opposite of Sonya if she'd tried.

"Fine," said Edgar. "Tora, Reed, Alec, Markus, Web, and Trent stay with James. I'll take Connor, Max, Becca, Tyler, Ian, and Bez."

I wished I could see everyone in the dark. Some names were familiar, like Trent and Ian who had guarded the bar, and Web, the husky guy I'd met earlier with Reed, but others weren't. Our group would be on Markus' ship and the rest would stay on Max's.

"I'll take first shift out here for us." Edgar called to our group. "Web, how 'bout you take first shift for you guys?"

"Yep," said Web. "Sure thing."

"I'm happy to go with Reed's group too," a voice called from the dark.

"Thanks, Connor," said Edgar. "But I think we've got it worked out." Connor had been the one who'd questioned Edgar at the meeting. Strange that he'd care about being in my group.

"Let's go," said Reed, pulling on my arm. "I'm famished and tired, in that order."

I'd never been so happy to see Markus' ship, though it was hardly visible, not just because of the darkness, but because he'd made a great cover of leaves and branches to keep it hidden from the air. He had his flaws, but Markus was smart when it counted. I barely made it on board before Lucy ran up and slobbered all over me. She went down the line and made sure she greeted everyone in an equally messy way. I hoped everyone was fine with dog saliva. Alec and Markus had taken down a meat monster while they were waiting for us, and they all dug in. I could hardly choke down a bite.

Alec handed me some water. "At least drink this."

"Thanks." With the ocean of tears I'd cried, I'm sure I was dehydrated.

Web stood guard outside, while those inside ate and shared stories about the Resistance and how it had changed since they'd arrived on Caelia.

"I swear Kale used to be a live-and-let-live kind of guy," Trent said. "It wasn't until we got to Caelia that he started sounding a little *loco*."

Kale had been *loco* well before coming to Caelia, but I kept my mouth shut and sipped my water. He probably hoped that one day *his* name would be used as a swear word. The scent of the meat was became too tempting and I asked for some. Reed passed it to me, and I picked a piece off a bone and popped it into my mouth. "Do we know exactly what we're up against with Kale? Like how many men he has behind him?" I asked.

"Hard to say for sure," said Trent. "He has at least four hard-core soldiers, along with one guy who pilots for him. They're the same crew that busted out your dad." He frowned. "It's hard to tell how many more supporters he has here in Callie City though."

Reed couldn't stop petting Lucy and gushing over how cute she was, which didn't seem to bother Lucy in the least. Alec beamed like a proud papa.

"I just love this dog," she said. "Hope you don't mind, but while you were undercover at the Consulate, I used to sneak her food when James tied her up outside the bar."

Alec laughed. "I'm just glad she was so well taken care of by everyone."

After scarfing down all her scraps, Lucy laid her head in Reed's lap. Reed sat with her back against the ship wall, her head tipped back and eyes heavy. Alec scooted closer so she could lean against him.

Poor Markus, I thought. I didn't know if he'd realized Becca was on the other ship.

After a while, James ordered a shift change, and Trent went out to relieve Web. My head was barely staying upright and a deep heaviness weighed on my bones. Even Markus looked tired. "Anyone else feeling the need for some shut-eye?" he asked.

"Great idea," James said. "Everyone should get some rest until we switch out again." He looked at me pointedly. "Especially you."

Markus stretched and lay on the floor using his arm as a pillow. "Tora, you can take the sleep chamber in my room. I'll be fine out here."

I was too tired to protest.

James helped me up and we walked to Markus' room. I yawned. "What about you?" I asked. "You need rest too."

James pulled back the cover so I could climb in. "Not in the cards for me right now. I'll check on you in a bit." He leaned over and pulled the cover up to my chin. "Get some sleep," he said and kissed me lightly.

I fought, but my limbs felt like leaden weights.

My eyes closed and my mind drifted.

Dad was walking toward me with a stack of burning notebooks.

Crashing and shouts woke me and, in my sleep-induced haze, I momentarily forgot where I was. The room was dark, and I felt for the light panel with one hand while reaching for my gun with the other. The lights buzzed on.

The door opened, and James pushed Reed and Lucy inside. "You stay here until I get back. Don't open the door for anyone." He turned the light panel back off and secured the door before I could even ask what was happening.

"What's going on?" I asked Reed.

"We don't know. There were laser blasts outside the ship."

Kale attacking at night seemed unlikely, but he wasn't the most predictable guy in the world.

I turned to Reed. "Do you have a gun?" I whispered.

"Of course," she said. "I might not love guns, but they're part of the job description here.

I hit the light panel again. "Then why the hell are we in here?"

Reed's face was pale. "I'm not gonna lie. I'm scared to

death. But even I'll admit that staying here is a waste of two guns." She powered up her weapon. "If you're in, I'm in."

I powered up my own gun as we opened the door. Lucy tried to follow us, but I stopped her. "Sorry, girl. Stay here and we'll be back."

We walked to the main area of the ship where everyone had been eating not long before. It was deserted. They must all be outside. I pushed the hatch door open and booked it to the nearest tree. Reed followed close behind. We could hardly see anything under the heavy cloud cover. That is, until a laser blast flashed through the trees just up ahead by Max's ship.

"We need to get closer," I whispered to Reed. I took a breath and raced from one tree to another until we were near where I'd seen the blast. My heart thudded in my chest. *Where was everyone?* Someone ran up behind me and I stifled a scream.

"Do you listen to anything I say?" James asked in a low voice.

"Only when it's not sexist. Are you kidding me with the whole 'saving the women and dog' thing?"

"That's not what I was doing," James said. "With everything you just went through with your dad, I didn't think you needed more trauma."

"My whole life has been a trauma. It's unavoidable. Now let's go."

Max's voice crackled through James' com device,

though he was barely audible. "Over here, behind my ship." Max mumbled another word that I didn't catch.

"Say that again," James said, holding the com up to his ear so he could hear better.

He waved his arm and several figures joined us. "Two by two, get behind the ship. Go." He grabbed my sleeve. "You're sticking with me."

Markus, Trent, and Web went first, followed by James and me. Alec and Reed brought up the rear. A laser blast shot past my head, and I dove and rolled behind a tree.

"Who is it?" I asked when James rushed to my side. "Is it Kale? What did Max say?"

"Kale's probably behind this, but I don't think that's who's shooting at us. We have to get to Max fast. I think he's hurt."

Max had gone out of his way to help us and I wanted to return the favor. "Why do you think that? What did Max say?" Another round of lasers flashed through the night.

"Just one word," said James. "Mutiny."

Chapter SEVENTEEN

Adrenaline pumped through me as we raced toward Max's ship. He hadn't had time to camouflage it, so at least it was visible in the dark—the hull gleamed. We were close to the ship when another laser flashed nearby. Alec yelled and stumbled. James fired in the direction of the last blast and a male voice screamed in agony.

"You okay, Alec?" James called.

"*Sí.* I've been better, but I should make it," he said. "Don't think I can walk, though."

Reed bent over him. "Keep going," she said. "I'll watch over Alec."

"I'll help her drag him behind a tree," Web said. "I'll be right back."

The rest of us sprinted the last hundred yards and rounded the back of Max's ship. He sat on the ground, half-leaning against the hull. James shrugged off his pack as he leaned down to get a better look. I got to my knees and held Max's hand. His eyes were half-closed and blood ran down his neck toward the ground.

Markus let out a low whistle. "Oh wow, that doesn't look good."

"Talk to me, Max," James said and grabbed a vial from the bag. "Markus, turn the light on your com and hold it over us so I can see."

Trent stood guard while James worked on Max. His voice came out garbled and weak. The only word I understood was "pain."

"I'm going to give you something for the pain and to help stem the bleeding," James said. He administered the first vial around the gaping wound on Max's neck. It looked like the blue withdrawal med vial, but was red. I remembered the pain tabs we'd had in our medical kit in the bunker. Max must have needed something stronger that would give more immediate relief. The e-stitching tool I'd seen James use before was on top of the pack.

"Can't you just use that thing the way you did on Kale's leg?" I asked.

James shook his head but didn't say anything. He dug into his bag and pulled out a different colored vial along with a small device that had a wide, flat disk on top. "Hang in there," he said as he powered up the device and pressed the disk directly against the gash. "This will feel really hot, but will cauterize the wound and stop the bleeding."

Max whimpered despite the pain medication. I

squeezed his hand. "It's okay. We're right here with you. You're going to be fine."

James administered the second vial near the major artery on the uninjured side of Max's neck. "This helps your blood cells to replenish faster. You've lost a lot of blood."

Web ran back. "Alec is stable, but he could use some of your medical mojo when you're finished here." He finally took a good look at Max. "Oh god, Max, you look like crap. We need you, man, so do whatever the doc here says."

I shifted and the stench of blood filled my nostrils. My stomach churned and bile rose in my throat. Maybe there was only so much blood that someone could take in a day. I turned my head to avoid gagging in Max's face. After several deep breaths, I regained control of myself.

"Markus and Tora, stay here," James ordered. "Web, take Trent, and go see what kind of shape that guy who shot Alec is in."

Web checked his gun. "And if he's not in bad shape, should I make him that way?"

"No. We need info on who's behind this. Make him talk first."

"And after?" Web asked. His hulking frame made me glad I wasn't the one he was going after.

James didn't hesitate. "They betrayed us and tried to kill our men. End him."

James probably thought I'd considered that cruel, but it was hard to disagree, when I was sitting with a guy missing half his throat.

"Then find the others from Max's ship. There was more than one person firing lasers out there." James sat back on his heels and studied his com device, while Web and Trent took off.

"What are you doing?" I asked.

"Waiting. Timing the med in his system. I need to give it a few minutes."

Max mumbled again. "Thirsty."

I knew how thirsty he must be but doubted the water would even make it past the hole in his neck. "Should I try to find him some?" I asked.

"Not yet. Max, I'm gonna get you water as soon as I can. We just need to get this fixed up first."

Several lasers flashed near where I'd almost been hit earlier. Brief shouts, followed by silence. I stared at the com, hoping to hear a familiar voice.

James pressed a small cylindrical device into Max's neck and pushed a button. It looked like a med vial, but bigger.

"Ow," Max said, though his voice sounded a little clearer.

James pulled it back and examined the numbers that flashed across it. "I just got a sample of blood. Red cell count is low, but rising. Another minute and we'll try to close this up."

No word from the men and even James looked anxious as he watched his silent com device. The sound of lasers would be better than the quiet—it would mean at least some of our guys were still alive.

Trent and Web returned, breathless. "I think we got 'em all," Web said as he gasped for air.

"Yeah," said Trent. "That first guy, the one you shot, James, he was already a goner when we got there. One of Kale's cronies."

"The main traitor was Connor." Web holstered his gun. *Connor.* The one who'd tried to switch to my group. "He said it's a crime to destroy weapons that powerful. It took a little persuasion, but he let it spill that Kale ordered them to take out all of us except James and Tora."

Why would Kale want me spared? He knew James could fire the guns and was more than fine with killing me before.

James just shook his head as he picked up the electronic stitching device. "Okay, Max, we're gonna give this a shot." He moved the device along Max's wound while Max gritted his teeth and grunted in pain.

I didn't want to ask. I did anyway. "Is Connor dead?"

Web shrugged. "He is now. It was just the two of them. Sounds like the plan was for Kale to return with his pilot and the rest of his men at the light break to retrieve you two 'prisoners'."

The last thing I ever wanted to be was Kale's prisoner again. I'd rather face another meat monster.

James finished the stitching and set the device down. "Where are the others from Max's ship?"

Trent looked down. "I didn't see them."

Max squeezed my hand and took a deep breath. "Edgar is dead. He's inside." He took another breath. "They went for him first, probably because he was the strongest fighter." He looked down at the ground. "There's blood everywhere."

I hadn't known Edgar long, but I'd miss him, so I couldn't imagine how the others must be feeling.

"I'm so sorry, Max. Hey, you're talking!" Hearing him able to speak gave me hope. "How do you feel?"

Max swallowed. "Lucky."

James took another scan of Max's blood. "Counts are still rising. The bleeding must have mostly stopped. Take it easy for the next few hours though—you don't want this to tear open again."

"Got it. Thanks, James. I'm fine if you want to check on Alec now." Max looked up at Web. "No word about Becca, Tyler, Ian, or Bez?"

Web shook his head. "No sign of them. It's too dark to see much but we'll check later when the light hits."

I helped Max to his feet. He was a little unsteady and leaned on me so hard that I stumbled. Markus ran over and slung Max's other arm around his neck.

"Tora, can I talk to you a sec?" James asked.

Web stepped in and took Max's arm while I met James by the side of the ship. "What's up?"

He looked serious. "I want you, Markus, and Web to

take Max back to Markus' ship. I'll take Trent to check out Alec. Stay on guard and don't let your gun out of your sight."

"Okay." I touched his arm. "What you did with Max there was impressive."

James shook his head. "Honestly, I didn't think it would work. I thought he was done. I'm serious about not letting him move around too much. He's not in the clear yet."

James gripped my hand. "I'll meet you back at the ship once I have Alec fixed up. Be careful."

I nodded. "You too. Don't take too long." I went back over to Markus. "Let's get Max back to your ship. He needs to rest."

The sky was tinged with gray light as we made our way back. Even with the traitors eliminated, there was an uneasiness in the air. It was completely silent aside from our breathing. The lasers must have frightened away any animals in the area. I walked in front of Markus and Web, who supported Max, helping him to walk. My gun was powered up and pointed into the murky space ahead.

Clouds still covered most of the sky, but it grew lighter as the sun pushed up toward the horizon. I could just make out the shape of the ship in the distance beneath its giant leaf cover. As we reached our destination, I froze. I signaled Markus to stop.

The outline of a figure stood just outside the hatch door. My gun hummed reassuringly in my hand. I crept around the side of the ship. "Don't move or I'll shoot," I said in my best no-nonsense voice.

"Go ahead. I'm so tired of this. I don't even know who's on what side anymore," a girl answered.

"Are you Becca?" I asked and stepped closer. I noticed the blood dripping down her arm.

She nodded. "That's about all I do know. Well that, and that Connor is a freakin' burner."

I lowered my gun. "He's dead if that helps you feel any better."

She sniffed. "It does, thanks. Can I hide out in here with you? "

I turned behind me and called out to Markus and the others. "It's okay. Becca is alive."

They approached the ship, and Web gave Becca a big hug while Markus opened the hatch door. "Where's Tyler?" Web asked.

Becca shook her head and stifled a sob. "Ty's dead. He jumped in front of Connor's laser when he was aiming for me." She turned her bloodied arm toward Web. "Thanks to Ty the laser just skimmed my arm. I fired back and got Connor in the leg, but Ty was already gone. Edgar's gone too. Don't know what happened to Ian and Bez."

"Tyler was a good guy," Web said. He put his arm around Becca. "If it helps, your hitting Connor made it easier for us to get him. He couldn't run very far, and we closed in."

Markus settled Max into one of the passenger chairs

inside the ship. I'd considered putting him on the sleep pad but thought it might be better for his neck if he stayed upright. I found him a bottle of Caelia Pure.

He started to chug it, and I had to pull it away. "Easy now," I warned. "You don't want to put any additional strain on your throat. There's plenty of water."

Max sighed. "I'm just so thirsty."

"I know. I've been there." I eased the bottle to his mouth. "Just little sips for now, though, okay?"

He swallowed a few more times. "That's better," he said. He looked up at me. "You know I should be dead now, right? James saved my life and I could tell that even he seemed surprised by that."

I nodded. It's good he hadn't been able to see the extent of the damage to his throat. Max reached up tentatively to touch his wound and I slapped his hand away. "Don't do that. You heard James—leave it alone for a few hours to make sure it heals right."

Web sat on the floor near us and pressed a clean cloth against Becca's arm. "It's not too bad," he told her. "Little more than a nasty scratch, really."

Markus smiled at me and patted the floor next to him. "Take a load off, sweetcakes. Nothing to do but wait for now."

I scooted next to Markus and let my head fall against his shoulder. The only feeling I knew lately was tired. Web comforted Becca who broke into tears from time to time, while Max fell into a much-needed sleep. At one point, his head lolled to the side and I worried it would tear his neck open, but Markus followed my stare and patted my hand in reassurance. Just as my eyelids threatened to close, I glanced out the window. The sky had a pinkish-orange cast to it, tendrils of light threading their way through the gray.

I jumped to my feet. "Where are they? Why aren't they back yet?" Kale and his men would be back at any moment if they weren't already. "C'mon, Markus, we have to get James and the rest of them."

Max stirred, but didn't wake. I looked down at Becca. "Stay here with Max, okay?"

"Where do you want me?" Web asked.

"Near the door," said Markus. "That way, if we're in trouble you can keep the hatch open for us."

Markus and I powered up our guns and ran out into the dawn. For someone who despised running, I'd done more of it in the last year than in my entire life combined. Once this was all over, running was going into my file of "Things I Never Want to Do Again."

We only made it about a hundred yards before we saw Alec hobbling toward us with James and Reed. Ian and another guy—Bez, I guessed—were with them. Relief shot through me.

They got closer. "Hey," said James. "Found Ian and Bez heading our way. Told them what happened with Max."

"Glad you guys are okay," Markus said.

"It's good to be okay, but I wish Edgar was too. Hey,

I'm Bez . . . you must be Tora. Sorry I couldn't be at the meeting." He extended his hand.

I shook it and looked at Alec. "How is he?" I whispered, not sure if Kale might have already landed near the woods.

"It was worse than he thought," said James. "But I think he'll be fine."

"No burnin' laser is going to keep me down," said Alec with a grin. Reed had her arm linked through his. Despite being injured, he sure looked happy.

"Becca's alive," I said. "She has a slight injury."

"And Tyler?" Ian asked.

I shook my head. "Tyler died saving her."

"That sounds like him," said James. "Those two were tight. She okay?"

Markus answered. "I'm gonna say no. She keeps bursting into tears right as I'm trying to get some shut-eye. You got meds for that?"

"Just pain meds, but all they'll do is make her tired."

I thought about Kale's drunken reaction to the meds back in the bunker on Earth after his leg was injured. "Why didn't the meds affect Max the way they did Kale?"

James smiled. "I might have given Kale way more than he needed."

Markus grimaced at me. "I can't believe I ever got it on with her. All that crying and whining . . . geez. I like my girls a little tougher than that."

A bomb could be dropping overhead and Markus would still be assessing hookups.

Web waved to us from the hatch. "Ian, Bez, right on! Glad you guys made it back."

A ship roared overhead. Since Alec couldn't move quickly, I ran to protect the group from behind. Markus sprinted for the door. Kale would see us if he was flying low enough. I dared a peek upward. The ship passed overhead followed seconds later by another ship, and another. I stared in horror as they went by. It wasn't Kale.

It was the Consulate.

Chapter EIGHTEEN

"CONSULATE!" I SCREAMED. "GET INSIDE."

James encouraged Alec to lean on him, while Ian and Bez helped to get him to the door. Reed reluctantly let go of Alec's arm so the others could help him to safety. As soon as we got inside the hatch, Markus closed the door. I ran to the window. The sky was clear—no sign of the Consulate ships that had passed over. Lucy whined as she circled anxiously around all of us, stopping to lick the dried blood on Alec's leg.

"It's okay, girl," Alec said. He sat down and let Lucy curl up in his lap. Ian and Bez exchanged back-slaps with Trent.

Just when I thought maybe the ships hadn't seen us, one of them circled back. Though Markus' ship would be hard to spot from the air thanks to the camouflage, Max's probably looked like a nice, shiny target, right along with the bar and command center. I looked down in frustration at the standard-issue gun in my hand. A crap load of help it would be against the Consulate.

"What the hell do we do?" I asked.

There was a moment of silence followed by the whine of the first bomb. The explosion was deafening and the ground shook under the ship. It had to be nearby, and I wondered which target was gone.

Markus groaned. "This is a load of déjà vu crap. I could've lived my whole life without going through this hell all over. And it's not like we even have a bunker door to hide behind."

"What's going on?" Max rubbed his eyes and stood up on wobbly legs.

"We're under attack," James said. Trent, Ian, Bez and Web stood at attention as though waiting for orders.

Becca burst into tears again, and Alec and Reed tried to comfort her. Markus leaned in toward me. "Seriously, what the hell was I thinking? Emotional and fragile is really not my type."

I smacked him. "We've got bigger problems here, you know?"

"I know," he said. "Shame you don't have those über-guns, huh?"

James met my eyes. "If Kale thought an attack was imminent, he wouldn't have hidden the guns far away. It wouldn't make sense. Not if he planned for you and me to help him fight the Consulate."

"But Sonya implied that the guns were somewhere romantic, or that Kale took her somewhere romantic at least," I said. "The only place I can think of that fits that description is the beach, but it's not like he'd bury the guns in the sand."

"Wait, Sonya said the guns were somewhere romantic?" James asked.

"Yeah, I told you that. Oh no, wait, I heard that at the command center meeting . . . Why?"

James looked sheepish. "She mentioned a few times that she'd love for me to give her a private tour of Kale's ship when he got back. Something about the Resistance leader's ship being a turn-on or something."

"Shame she's on the wrong side," said Markus. "She is so my kind of girl."

"Knock it off. She's a total burner. Also, she obviously likes men in power. Your drunk-and-falling-down routine probably didn't impress her much."

"I'm a changed man," said Markus. "Maybe we can convert her."

The image of Sonya walking her fingers up James' arm was seared forever in my brain. But what sealed her fate was her role in Dad's murder. "We're not converting her. We're killing her."

"Fine," said Markus, "but I get to kill Kale for what he did to Britta."

It was the first time I'd heard him acknowledge what had happened. Either James had told him the truth or he'd figured it out on his own.

"Back to the point," James said. "The guns have to be on his ship. Wherever that is."

"Can you find his com channel?" I asked.

"He's always used a protected channel. We'll have to find the actual ship."

Trent sighed. "If he saw the Consulate ships, he wouldn't come anywhere near here. Wouldn't he just wait for them to blow us all up?"

The answer had just hit me. "He thinks his only chance to take out the Consulate once and for all is with those guns. He needs us."

James nodded. "His entire mission is revenge. He won't be afraid of them."

"So if he's looking for you two, where would he look?" Ian asked.

"He didn't know where our camp was," James said. "Best guess would be the bar or command center."

"Which are probably blown to smithereens," noted Markus.

"It's worth a shot," I said. "Kale and company might be in that area at least."

James surveyed the lot of us. "The injured stay here—Max, Alec, and Becca. Trent and Bez, you guys watch over them in case something goes wrong. Keep in touch through the com."

"Wouldn't it be better to have more able-bodied persons helping out?" Reed asked. She shot a glance at Alec.

"I mean, I could stay too."

Her reluctance to come with us was about more than wanting to be with Alec. I'd seen the fear in her eyes before when she realized she'd actually have to use her gun.

"Sorry," said James. "We need all the help we can get in case there are Consulate forces on the ground."

Alec smiled at her. "I'd go if I could walk on my own. At least I've got Lucy. She's a pretty tough soldier herself." Lucy licked his hand in agreement.

Max was a little more steady on his legs than before. "I want to help. I'm feeling better."

I shook my head. "I appreciate that, but after all the work James did to bring you back, you're going to sit here and you're going to like it."

James raised an eyebrow as he double-checked his weapon. "Listen to the lady, Max. You're no good to us dead."

Fresh sobs erupted from Becca. "I don't want to die."

Web looked grateful that he wasn't the one assigned to stay behind. Like he'd rather face Consulate soldiers than comfort Becca for another minute. How she ever got to be a member of the Resistance was beyond me. Ian just looked angry, like he wanted revenge.

"We ready?" James asked.

Web and Ian snapped to attention. "Ready, sir."

"Sure," said Markus, twirling his gun in his hand. "Let's get this over with."

Reed came and stood by my side. "I hate this part."

I nodded. "Me too." But I was grateful that we didn't have to put on sunsuits and worry about our oxygen supply on top of everything else.

Markus opened the hatch and we filed out into the daylight. Another bomb dropped in the distance and the ground shook so much that I fell to my knees.

"You okay?" asked Reed.

I dusted myself off as I stood up. "Never better." All I wanted was to lie in the soft, pink sand again with James at my side. Instead, I was traipsing through the woods after Kale and the Consulate. A girl couldn't catch a break.

Markus put a finger to his lips. We were supposed to be silent in case of ground troops.

"Look at you being all rule-abiding," I whispered in annoyance.

His smug expression made me want to punch him. I hoped he wasn't trying to impress Reed, because it was pretty clear she had a thing for Alec.

It was warm outside but the clouds remained despite the light break. The sun peeked through once or twice. A gray pall enveloped everything and a heavy mist hung in the air. We decided to head straight for the bar since it was the closest building.

James and Web walked in front of Reed and me. Markus and Ian hung back behind us. The burned-out hull of Max's ship smoked ahead. It had taken a direct hit.

"Maybe it's not a bad thing," said Reed in a low voice. "With all of them dead on there."

"Yeah, just a shame for Max to lose his ship." I know how Markus felt about his ship, and assumed it was probably the same for Max. It was an even stronger bond than I'd felt about my first gun, Trigger.

No birds chirped and those pretty winged insects were nowhere in sight. They'd probably fled from the destruction. Those Consulate burners were already destroying a whole new planet. They'd never stop. Unless someone stopped them.

Reed leaned over and spoke in a conspiratorial whisper. "So, I was just wondering about Alec—"

Another bomb hit not far away and reverberations rippled through the trees. I steadied my legs to keep from falling again.

"What else is there left to hit?" I asked. They must have taken out the bar and command center by now.

"The camps," said James.

I hoped the Resistance was smart enough to avoid the camps and that the Consulate was bombing nothing but empty huts.

I realized that now that the Consulate had Dad's trigger formulas, they wouldn't need me alive. Killing everyone related to the Resistance would be their goal.

Soon enough we reached what once was the bar. It had burned to the ground. Guess there were downsides to building with wood instead of thermoplastic.

"No sign of Kale. Should we move on to what's left of the command center?" I asked.

"Yeah," said James. "Steer clear of open areas so we're not seen from above."

We kept to the densest cover. We'd made it halfway to the command center when Kale and Sonya stepped out from behind a group of trees.

"About time you showed up," Kale said, casually examining his weapon. "I've got some guns I was hoping you could use."

James and I exchanged glances. From Kale's matter-of-fact tone, you'd never know that he'd just murdered my father. I'd play along for now. Act like I had no idea my dad was dead. Act like Kale hadn't gone to great lengths to have me killed a few short months before.

I'd do anything to get my hands on one of my weapons and take him down for good. I'm sure he wished the same about me. The fact that I was thinking more like Kale bothered me, but I couldn't help that I hated him so much.

Markus clenched his fists. I reached out and patted his arm. It wasn't time yet.

"Nice to see you again too," I said.

Kale's smile was forced and his cheerful tone couldn't have been more fake. But you had to give him credit for having ginormous balls. "Tora, let's let bygones be bygones, water under the bridge, as people used to say on Earth. We've got Consulate burners after us and I think we have a chance if we all work together. What do you say?"

"Why should we trust you?" I asked. "You and I have had a bit of a rocky relationship—"

That was the understatement of the year. Like saying Earth had been water-challenged.

Kale held out in hands in a gesture of goodwill. "—but I think we can get past it. We both want the Consulate off our backs, once and for all, and I have guns that can make that happen . . . if you're willing to use them. Then we can go our separate ways and pretend this never happened."

I loved how he called the stolen guns *his*. Whatever. He wasn't going to live long enough to go anywhere once I was done with him. I forced a smile. "Well, Kale, that sounds like a deal that benefits all of us. It's so nice to be on the same side again. I hope these weapons of yours are nearby."

Sonya looked briefly at James, confusion and hurt in her face. Even a hint of guilt. I bet she hadn't fully realized what she was getting into with Kale. She must have felt my gaze because she turned and fixed her eyes on me. Her demeanor changed and she looked as though she could impale me with a stare.

Kale turned. "No time to waste. Follow us."

Ian shot James a questioning look.

"Let's go with them," said James. "We'll all stick together for now."

I glanced at James and he nodded slightly. We understood each other. As soon as we had the guns, we'd take them down. We hurried after Kale and didn't have to go far before we arrived at his ship, which had been buried under several large branches. His men stood guard. Kale opened the hatch and motioned to James and me. "Just you two."

Web walked up next to us. "Bad idea," he said to James under his breath.

"It's fine," James said. "We'll be right back."

I frowned. Splitting up in the past hadn't worked out so well for Britta, but James raised an eyebrow at me. He seemed confident in what was about to happen. We approached the ship and Kale waved James and me on board. "After you."

Sonya and Kale's pilot tried to follow us but Kale stopped them. "No need, soldiers, you can wait out here with the others."

I'm not sure whether it was the fact that he relegated her to standing with his other men or the fact that he called her "soldier," but the look on Sonya's face was murderous.

As I stepped through the hatch door, panic gripped me. The last time I'd been here, I'd run for my life back out this hatch—away from James—and onto a strange, shifting planet. My heart thudded as I tried to calm myself. I wasn't much safer this time around, but I'd take anything over James pointing a gun at me again.

Kale took us to the same small room where Britta had once forced me inside a human transport container. I actually missed that scrappy girl, though I'm sure not as much as Markus.

The containers of guns were stacked against the wall. Dad's guns. I walked over and dug through them. James came up to my side but remained silent.

My eyes fell on Trigger and memories flooded back. All the times I practiced with Dad as he showed me how to aim with precision and, later, after my family was gone, sitting with Trigger, my sole companion, and yearning for a way off Earth. How pathetic that memories of fighting for survival were the "good ole days." As much as I loved Trigger, I needed something powerful, something like my favorite boulder-killing gun, B.K. I'd blown so many rocks to bits with that gun, and then James had turned it against me.

"Hey?" I asked James. "Whatever happened to B.K. after you shot me with it?"

James looked at me like I was a petulant child. "Haven't we been over this? I never shot you with B.K. I only shot you with *my* gun."

I crossed my arms. "It never sounds good when you start a sentence with 'I only shot you with . . .'"

"Wait, you didn't shoot her with the super-gun?" Kale asked.

Oh, crap. Kale stood in the entrance watching James carefully. By now, Sonya would have told him about James being named the new Resistance leader.

"No," said James. It was the first time I'd ever heard him speak to Kale without calling him "sir." "I shouldn't have even shot her with my gun. It was stupid."

Wow. He wasn't even pretending to be on Kale's team anymore. That was terrifying and awesome all at once.

"Interesting," Kale said. He must hate the fact that he

couldn't kill us both right then and there.

James turned back to me. "The bomb you used on that crazy planet, what was it called again?"

"The Obliterator. T.O. Why?" How could I forget the weapon that blew up everyone around us except for James and me? I rifled through another container in my search of the most lethal gun I could find.

"I must have dropped B.K. in the seconds between the Consulate shooting me and you using T.O. The bomb didn't just take out all the Consulate soldiers and their ship—it took out everything in a several-mile radius. When that other ship landed and picked us up, the only gun in my hands—which they quickly confiscated—was my own. B.K. was nothing but a pile of dust."

I remembered how my satchel had survived the bomb because I'd been wearing it at the time, so it made sense that James' gun remained unscathed. What I hadn't realized was that T.O. would destroy the super guns too. Dad had truly designed the bomb as a last resort weapon. All along, I'd been trying to find a way to get rid of the weapons, when I could have just brought the lot of them to a location miles away from the nearest person and then detonated T.O. But T.O. was gone now, and there was nothing else like it in existence. Nothing else that could vaporize everything all at once.

Several of the guns looked similar to B.K., and I lifted a few of them from the box. Since Dad hadn't thought I'd need to keep using the guns, most of our training sessions had just been with Trigger and B.K. He'd only shown me how to use T.O. once, right before he left for his meeting with the Consulate and never came back.

"These should do," I said. I took two of the B.K.-like guns for myself. It would end now. We'd kill Kale, take the guns, and get out of here. The plan could still work. But Kale had to think we were working with him. I handed two other über-weapons to James, and said loudly, "Here, we need all the help we can get against the Consulate."

My eyes caught Trigger again and I set my two super-guns on the floor. I took the standard-issue gun out of my waistband and replaced it with Trigger. Between Kale and the Consulate, I didn't feel like I could ever have enough guns. There was something comforting about having Trigger at my side. It was like a reunion with a beloved childhood friend. I picked up the super-guns and faced James.

I tried to silently communicate to him that we needed to kill Kale now. As long as there weren't Consulate soldiers on the ground, we didn't need Kale or his men to help us fight. We exchanged a brief look. I acted nonchalant as I hit the buttons on the guns to power them up. Kale was about two seconds away from being a past problem rather than a current one.

An explosion rocked the ship and threw us to the floor. Flames shot out from the wall behind me. Kale yelled from the hatch, "Get out, the ship's gonna blow."

James grabbed my arm and we scrambled for the door.

We dove out into the woods just as the ship erupted into a huge fireball.

"This way," Kale shouted and we followed his men and Sonya into the woods.

Markus called to us through the com. "Where are you guys? You okay?"

We gave him our location and watched through the trees as the blaze reached toward the sky before it died down. Kale had no ship anymore, which meant that Markus had the only working Resistance ship left. Wonder how long it would take before Kale tried to take it for his own use.

The others found us a few minutes later.

"That was close," Markus said.

"Too close," said Web.

"Yeah," said Ian. "What's the plan?"

Though he looked at James, Kale answered. "We've got three ships to worry about. Two have been flying around dropping bombs, so I'm thinking the third one landed and sent out ground troops. You can bet that they'll be heading for that." He pointed through two large trees at the remains of his ship. Everything was still smoking and burning, including the containers that held the guns. The guns, themselves, were perfectly intact, though. Dad wasn't kidding when he told me that he'd made them completely heat-resistant in order to withstand the scorching sun of Earth. They lay among the wreckage in gleaming piles, a sure beacon for the Consulate soldiers.

My heart dropped. No matter what else happened, the Consulate couldn't get the guns. I didn't know how long it would take them to figure out the missing steps to rekey the triggers, but once they did, we wouldn't have a chance at survival. We had to protect those weapons.

"We should spread out in the woods around the perimeter," said James. "Once a Consulate ship flies back over and sees the guns, they'll alert the ground troops."

"We'll work together," said Kale. "I'll send a few of my men with each of you."

Of course. He wanted to keep tabs on the guns . . . and us. I'd bet anything that his men had orders to kill us as soon as the Consulate threat was over.

As much as I didn't want to split up, I knew what we had to do.

What I had to do.

"I'll stay here," I said. There was no way I was letting the guns out of my sight. "I'll go after any ship that comes this way." I swallowed hard. "James, are you thinking the same thing I am?"

He nodded. "It's the only thing that makes sense. Markus' ship is all we have left, and we have to protect the people on board. I'll go there with a few men." The fact that he said it out loud, even though Kale would soon know the location of the ship, meant he didn't plan on Kale living long enough to do anything with that information. If we made it out of this alive, I was going to show James exactly how brilliant I thought he was.

Kale nodded and selected his pilot, another man, and Sonya, to go with James. Of course he picked Sonya.

"I'll stay here," Kale said.

Yay for me. I got to hang out with the person I most wanted to kill, while the person I wanted to be with more than anything was leaving.

Maybe it was a good thing I was stuck with Kale. Killing him would be the highlight of my week. Well, aside from my beach time with James.

"I'm staying with Tora," Markus said. "I've got my com so I can stay in touch with you."

James nodded. "Good idea. Web, you stay here too. Reed and Ian can come with me."

Reed looked like she wanted to jump for joy. I'm sure she wanted to get back to Alec as soon as possible. I knew the feeling and couldn't blame her for it, though I'd miss having her nearby. The fact that Markus was staying made me feel better. He'd have my back and keep an eye on Kale.

James placed his finger under my chin and tipped my face up toward his. "Stay safe."

"I'll try. Wait, here." I handed James my satchel with Callie's picture and the trigger formulas inside. "Keep this safe for me." I didn't trust having it on me when I was with Kale.

I ignored Kale's raised eyebrow and watched James head off with his group.

"Hey, James?" Markus called after the group.

James looked back. "Yeah."

"Take care of my bird," he said. "We've flown through a lot of crap together, and I'm sort of attached to her."

"I'll do my best." James disappeared into the trees, which swayed back and forth in the breeze.

I wondered if I'd see him again. I didn't have long to contemplate that thought when I heard the roar of a Consulate ship zooming back our way. If I hit it, taking it down on the first try, maybe the crew members aboard wouldn't get the chance to notify the other ships about finding the weapons.

"Cover me," I said to Markus and Web as I crept to the edge of the area where Kale's ship had been.

"You heard the woman," Kale said to his two men. "Get moving and cover her." Even he crouched down with his gun aimed upward.

The Consulate ship flew low, almost grazing the tops of the trees. It fired lasers as it went, and when it neared the clearing, a hatch slid open near the bottom of the hull. I didn't want to wait and see if we could survive a direct hit from another bomb. I jumped out into the open clearing with my gun raised. The ship dipped lower and I fired, but shot a second too late. Their bomb dropped at the same time that my laser hit the ship. I missed the engine, and instead I blasted off the entire nose. The ship veered sharply downward and crashed near the weapons as the bomb hit the edge of the tree line.

I dove into the woods as shrapnel from the ship and branches shot through the air. Thick flames and smoke filled the woods. I covered my head with my arms to protect myself from the onslaught of twigs and branches.

"Mengistu!"

I kept my head down and peeked behind me. Kale had a tree branch sticking straight out of his thigh. He yanked it out with a grunt and blood poured down his leg. I'd rather the branch had impaled his skull, but I'd take what I could get. At least James would be safe a while longer since Kale clearly needed medical attention.

When the aftershocks ended, I inspected my limbs for damage. Despite some good-sized cuts on my hands and arms, I was okay.

"We need to get to that downed ship, pronto," Kale said as he pressed on his leg with clumps of leaves to stop the bleeding.

I completely agreed with him, though I'd never admit it out loud. Even his "no survivors" policy sounded good to me. We had to hope the crash wiped out the com system so the Consulate soldiers couldn't signal for help.

"I'll be right behind you," Kale said as he tested out his leg and limped a few steps. "We'll be right back."

"Web, can you stay here in case anyone tries to go for the guns?" I asked.

Web held up his gun in a salute. "Yes, ma'am. No one will lay a hand on them on my watch."

Markus and I led the way with Kale's men close behind. Kale lagged and limped in the rear. We followed the smell of smoke for what must have been close to a mile as we headed toward the fallen ship. We'd check things out, then join the others at Markus' ship, so we could grab Web and the guns on our way out of here. Kale would have to die between now and then.

"At least we have the trees for cover," Markus said as we walked west.

No sooner had the words left his mouth than the smoke grew even thicker. The breeze kicked up and several embers blew past me. They landed in a tree to my left and the leaves caught fire. When I saw the flames up ahead through the trees, I stopped.

Markus stared at the sight in front of us, then took a step closer. He frowned. "Is the Consulate ship still on fire?" he asked.

The flames danced closer. "No," I said and tugged on his sleeve to pull him back toward me. "The forest is." I turned and yelled to the others, "Fall back. Fire!"

We ran back toward the area where we'd left Web guarding the guns. We'd have to take him with us to Markus' ship, or he'd get burned alive. The wind stoked the fire, and the flames fanned themselves out in a semi-circle as more embers were blown into the trees. Thick smoke burned my nostrils and made me cough. Fire was yet another thing that was faster than I was.

"Keep going this way," Markus called out. "We need to make it to the creek."

If the wind and fire kept going, I wasn't sure the creek would be wide enough to hold it back. The trees crackled around us as they were consumed by the fire, and I forced my legs to move faster. I checked behind me and Kale was barely keeping ahead of the flames. It would be a terrible way for him to die, but I couldn't help thinking that it would save me the trouble of killing him later.

Unfortunately, Kale's men stayed by his side and didn't seem to have plans to abandon him. When we reached where Kale's ship had been, I saw the sky. The wind had driven in some dark black clouds. Maybe that meant rain was coming. I'd seen Markus put out the fire in the fire pit by pouring creek water on it. The rain might do the same for the fire in the trees.

I scanned the clearing as I ran. The guns were there but Web was nowhere in sight. "Web!"

No response.

"Web!" I screamed again.

That's when I noticed a new sound above the pops and crackles of the trees—lasers.

"Go!" I shouted and ran toward the lasers firing on the opposite side of the clearing. Whoever was firing was between us and the safety of the creek. We had fire behind us and burners in front of us. Perfect.

Markus ran ahead of me and someone fired at him from the direction of the creek. It just missed him, and he dove and rolled behind the nearest tree. My lungs burned from the smoke and running, yet I made it into the trees on the east side of the clearing just as another laser fired.

There was return fire a second later but it didn't come from any of us.

I turned around and Kale and his men were dashing toward us, the forest ablaze behind them. They'd just passed the piles of Dad's weapons when more lasers blasted. Kale tried to dart to the side to avoid being hit but his injured leg gave out and he fell. The laser just missed him and hit one of his men instead. The man's body hit the ground in a heap. No medic would be necessary. Not even James' fancy gadgets could help someone without a head.

I motioned for Markus to follow me and we kept moving away from the fire toward the safety of the creek, even though it was the same direction the lasers had come from. That was when I felt the first drop of water. It was huge and splashed on my nose. Relief and fear competed with each other. The water would help with the fire, but I remembered what it did to my gun the last time. What if Dad's guns had the same reaction to water as the regular ones did? I remembered one time when he told me that he had to consider all future environments when designing the weapons, but would he have realized how wet some planets might be? I had to take care of these burners fast.

A laser shot my way and I ran straight toward it, firing my gun in rapid bursts. An arm reached out and yanked me back behind a tree.

"He'll kill you. Are you crazy?" Web asked.

I gasped. "Web! You're alive."

He grimaced. "For now."

I saw the blood on his arm. If I never saw more blood for the rest of my life, it would be too soon.

"How many are there?" I asked.

"Two for sure," he answered. "I got one, but I think he's still shooting."

Another raindrop hit my cheek. "Then let's stop him for good."

Markus ran up on my other side. "Sounds good to me. This crap is interfering with my nap schedule."

Web ran straight ahead while Markus and I flanked him. As another laser came toward us and hit a tree, the three of us fired in unison and didn't stop until we reached the spot where it had come from. A Consulate soldier lay on the ground, his gun still powered up and clutched in his dead hand. The heat coming from behind us told me the fire was still raging.

A groan came from nearby and I searched the trees for the source. The soldier sat against a tree, with a large laser blast hole through the abdomen of his Consulate uniform. When he tried to speak, no words came out and his gun was just out of his grasp. Markus ran up and grabbed the soldier's gun. He tossed it to Web who caught it and slipped it into his waistband.

"What do you think?" Web asked me.

An image of me as a younger girl flashed through my mind. It was the first time I ever held B.K., and I was sweating like crazy in my sunsuit. Dad pointed at a rock some distance away. "Kill him before he kills you, Tora. Just like I taught you." I'd hesitated and he'd grabbed the gun from my hand and blasted the rock to smithereens. Then he'd walked back to the bunker. As he opened the door, he shook his head. "If that had been a soldier, you'd be dead now."

The man writhed in pain on the ground. There was no way we'd be able to get any information out of him, and there was no way he'd survive.

I raised my gun and looked him straight in the eyes. "I'm sorry."

And I ended his pain.

Chapter NINETEEN

The occasional raindrops had settled into a steady, pitter-pat rhythm on the leaves. We ran toward the creek while Markus reported to James on the com that we'd taken down one Consulate ship as well as two ground soldiers who must have been from another ship. James said the fire hadn't reached them yet, though they could smell the smoke. He thought it would be best for Max to move the ship to a safer location.

As I ran, I kept thinking about the man I'd killed. Rather than guilt, I felt anger. Anger that the Consulate had started all of this crap. Anger that I was in the position of having to kill someone in the first place. Anger that I couldn't live out the rest of my life collecting seashells on the beach. And underneath it all, a tiny, nagging worry that I was becoming more like Kale.

I hadn't seen the second ship. It could have landed or

flown a different route, and there was a third ship out there somewhere. Markus handed me the com. I wished I was talking to James in person. "We're not too far from the creek," I said. "If Max flies Markus' ship to the other side, you should be safer from the fire. We can cover you from the ground if you fly straight over the clearing."

"Were you soldiers planning to wait for us or were you just hoping we would burn to death?" Kale came toward us doing a bizarre run-limp. His soldier kept glancing over his shoulder at the oncoming blaze and wore a look of terror on his face. The scattered raindrops had done nothing to subdue the inferno. Web ran in front of them. I got the sense he was acting as a buffer between Kale and me.

How was Kale not dead already? Between his leg, the fire, and the lasers, he should have been gone. If a meat monster attacked him out of nowhere, I had a feeling he would somehow escape unscathed. As soon as I knew we didn't need his help against the Consulate, I was so going to kill him if Markus didn't do it first.

I spoke into the com again. "Do it now. We've got other problems to deal with when you get there."

James' gravelly voice came through the com. "Don't do anything drastic. I'll be there soon."

For a second, everything disappeared, and it was like we were the only two people in the forest. I handed the com back to Markus. It was getting harder to keep up the same pace. My legs were tired. My ankle, which had felt great up until now, had started to hurt again. "Hey, your nap idea sounded really good back there, but think you could catch us a meat monster first once we're safe?"

Markus chuckled, though he sounded just as winded as I did. "Sure, I aim to please. And if you ever get tired of napping with James . . ."

I laughed. "Keep dreaming, soldier."

Over the next few hundred yards, the rain came down harder and harder, yet the fire raged on. My hair hung in heavy, wet curls around my shoulders. We finally reached the creek as a ship passed overhead. I figured it was Markus' until I looked up. The second Consulate ship zoomed past before I had a chance to fire. At first, I thought that maybe they'd seen Markus' ship, but they didn't fire. I craned my neck to look and the Consulate ship flew toward the very center of the blaze.

Something dropped from the ship, and I ducked and covered my head as I waited for the explosion. None came and I stood up, confused. A white hazy substance billowed up from the ground and headed in our direction.

"What are they doing?" Web asked.

The substance spread rapidly and was about to envelop us. "Maybe it's some kind of poison!" I screamed. I couldn't think what else it could be, but figured that between that and the fire, we'd be safest in the creek. "Get in the water."

We jumped into the stormy water, sticking close to the bank. I tried to hold my breath, but came up sputtering for air. Maybe I should have spent more time practicing my swimming after all. Web, Markus, and Kale's man were coughing in the water next to me, but with his hurt leg, Kale hadn't made it.

He stood on the bank, his body enveloped in white mist. He turned to us and rubbed his leg. "Well, I'm still standing, so it ain't poison."

Dumbfounded, I looked past him toward the trees. "The fire's out. They put the fire out with that stuff."

"That's it!" said Kale. "Flame extinguisher. I've heard of it being used before."

"Why?" asked Web.

Kale shrugged. "They're either trying to save their own or trying to get the guns. Either way, let's get the heck out of Dodge, people."

My stomach clenched as the Consulate ship circled back around toward us. Even with the mist, they'd have to notice a group of people standing in the creek. Just then Markus' ship, piloted by Max, headed straight for the creek. They were behind the Consulate ship and must not have seen them right away through the fog, because they suddenly pulled up and slowed down. The Consulate ship stopped and swiveled around. *God, no.*

I wiped the rain from my face and scrambled back on shore past Kale to the highest spot I could find. If I missed or accidentally hit Markus' ship, I'd never forgive myself. Please let Dad's guns work in the rain. The Consulate ship started firing before it had even fully locked on their ship.

"No!" I screamed. I aimed both guns and fired straight through the downpour.

I hit the engine dead center. The Consulate ship dove and headed full speed straight into the ground, still firing when it hit. Markus' ship sped away from the debris that catapulted from the wreckage. I ducked as a broken piece of the wing flew past my head and lodged into a tree. Flames shot up briefly from what remained of the ship, but the rain quickly doused them.

Markus came up, dripping wet from the creek, and clapped me on the shoulder. "Hey, good job, you finally hit an engine. Only took you a few ships but I think you've got it down now." He laughed. "Seriously, thanks for saving my bird."

Markus' ship passed overhead as a garbled voice came through the com. Markus attempted to wipe the water-logged device off with his shirt, but it was just as drenched.

". . . okay . . . over here . . . soon." It sounded like James.

Markus stuck the device in his pack. "This won't do us much good until it dries out. Let's head to the other side of the creek. They've got to be over there somewhere."

People were going to have to start inventing water-proof products if they planned to stay on Caelia long. The rain pounded down around us. I hoped the light flashes didn't start up again.

"Nice shooting there, soldier."

No way was he calling me soldier again. I'm sure it was only because there was one ship still out there. Otherwise, I'd be dead. "Thanks, Kale."

He slicked his hair back and shielded his eyes from the

torrential rain. "Where we heading?" I noticed that despite the rain and his injury, he'd managed to keep his gun in hand the entire time. His man stayed close to him.

"Across this creek," Web said. He eyed the Consulate embers. "Guess we don't need to worry about survivors with this one."

"No, and with the way that other ship caught fire, I'd doubt there are survivors there either," I said. "It's just a matter of how many are in that other Consulate ship."

I stared at the creek. It churned and the water level had risen so that it swelled and spilled over the banks.

Markus groaned. "This day just keeps getting better and better."

"Yeah," I said, "only the day part seems to be ending." It was hard to tell when the sun had started going down, but it was definitely getting darker.

"Great," said Markus, "now this crap is interfering with my mealtime." He leaned in toward me. "I get that we need Kale for now, but let me know the second I can take him out."

I nodded and secured Trigger by tying her tightly with the drawstring of my waistband then waded back into the creek, trying to keep the other two guns out of the water. Markus and Web followed. Markus cursed up a storm when his foot slipped, and he almost went under. Kale's man looked even less thrilled by the creek than he had by the fire and he stepped in with hesitation. Kale stomped into the water like it was just something else that annoyed him. His injury hadn't slowed him down as much as I'd hoped. For a second, I'd wondered if they'd desert us and go back for the guns, but they had no way to transport them. They needed Markus' ship for that.

The rushing water pulled against my body and it was hard to keep my footing. When I reached the center, the water came up to my chest. My arms burned from holding them up for so long. The guns were light but it would have been easier if I were taller.

A strong surge swept under me and my feet lost touch with the bottom of the creek. The water took me downstream, farther away from Markus and Web. I instinctively lowered one of my arms to try swimming and accidentally submerged the gun that was still in my hand. There was no way I could swim with a gun in each hand, so I let go of the one already underwater. With any luck, it would end up buried deep in the wet mud at the bottom of the creek.

I attempted a haphazard, one-armed stroke back to where Markus was barely visible through the rain. My brief swimming lesson hadn't prepared me for this. I wasn't getting very far very fast, inching along toward the bank and choking on water every few seconds. Thankfully, my toes brushed the bottom again and I was able to crawl through the water slowly.

"My gun!" Kale yelled.

He'd reached the center of the creek and must have lost his grip. His man ran downstream and felt around under the water, submerging his own weapon in the process.

After a minute, he fished Kale's gun out of the creek. "Got it, sir!"

I smiled as I trudged through the water, though my legs moved like clumsy weights. The wetter Kale's weapon, the better.

Markus reached the other side and called out, "Get over here, sweetcakes. Not a good time to go for a swim." When I got close enough, he reached out his hand and pulled me to him. I climbed up onto the slippery bank with the last remaining strength in my legs. It felt so good to be back on land. I made sure Trigger was still secured to my drawstring and kept the remaining B.K.-style gun in my hand.

Web climbed out shortly after I did. I hoped that a sudden surge would pull Kale under and drown him, but he marched up onto the bank safely. If I'd been even a teeny bit more like him, I would have killed him while he struggled. He still limped but the wound looked cleaner. The man thrived in extreme conditions. His soldier dragged himself up on the bank and rolled over on his back, exhausted.

The rain had let up a little, which helped, but the sky was growing darker by the minute. "Can we try the com again?" I asked Markus.

He held up his soaking wet pack in response. I sighed. "Damn. Let's walk fast then."

We moved toward the horizon. In the distance, I thought I saw a light flash. "Did you see that?" I asked.

"Where?" Markus asked.

It flashed again.

"I saw it," Web said. "Max must be sending a signal."

My heart leapt in relief. They were okay. My pace picked up. I'd see James soon. We headed toward the flashing light while I wondered how to handle the Kale situation when we got there.

The sound of firing lasers echoed in the distance, but they weren't coming from the direction of the flashing light. They came from behind us, back on the other side of the creek. I peered back into the twilight and could barely make out the lasers through the trees. There was no way we could recross the creek in time to help.

Web turned back to the flashing light. "I say we get to the light, find out what's going on, and then worry about all that. There's nothing we can do from here, anyway."

"Sounds like a plan," said Markus. "Have I mentioned I could eat an entire herd of meat monsters?"

My stomach turned. Despite not having eaten in a while, the idea of food didn't sit well. The stress had killed my appetite. "I'm sure they have stuff on the ship, even if it's just gel packets," I told him.

I looked skyward. It was full night, though clouds covered the moons and a steady drizzle still fell. The breeze had lessened, but every time it blew across my body I shivered in my wet clothes. Visions of a dry shirt—and James—kept me going. The light grew closer and voices permeated the darkness.

"Bez?" Web called. "Is that you, bro?"

A hulking figure, even larger than Web, ran toward us. "You guys made it!" Bez slapped Web on the back. "James had me out here to keep an eye out for you. The ship is back this way."

I did mental calculations as we walked. Aside from the guy with Kale, there were three more of Kale's men, including his pilot, with James. And Sonya. With Max and Alec injured, and Becca being Becca, that left James, Markus, Web, Trent, Bez, Ian, Reed and me. It wasn't perfect, but at least we outnumbered them.

"How is everyone?" Web asked Bez.

He paused. "Ian's dead. Some Consulate ground troops found Markus' ship just as James and the others were coming back. We got a few of them, just not before they got Ian."

"I'm so sorry," I said, my gut twisting. *How many more people had to die before this ended?*

"Yeah," said Bez. He sighed. "Max and Alec are doing okay, though. It helps that Reed is doting all over them. And Lucy is loving up everybody."

We walked through the hatch and James ran up, grasped my face in his hands, and kissed me. "You're awesome. You saved us," he said.

Kale's voice boomed from the entrance of the small ship. "How come I never got a greeting like that, soldier?" He rubbed his leg. "Makes a man feel underappreciated."

"Kale, your leg!" Sonya shrieked. She ran to him and looked at him the same way she'd looked at James the first time I saw her.

Markus leaned over and whispered, "Oh yeah, Kale definitely showed her his ship all right."

Reed came over and hugged me, while Lucy licked my arm. Alec waved from where he sat on the floor with his leg bound. Max was actually up and moving around. He looked great for someone that had his neck blown open not long ago.

"James, I saw laser fire back in the clearing where the weapons are," I said. "We need to get over there and help."

"Kale is the one that needs some help here," Sonya demanded.

James looked surprised. He completely ignored her. "That's a good sign. It means there are other Resistance members still out there. I heard them earlier but their coms must have gone out from the storm." He touched my sopping shirt. At least the thermoplastic wasn't translucent or I'd be giving everyone quite the show right now. "And you're soaked. Let's get you a dry shirt."

"My room, third drawer down," Markus said. "Grab me one while you're in there."

"Max, can you fly us over there?" James asked as he walked toward Markus' room. "The last Consulate ship is still out there, so we need to be quick." He turned back to Kale. "I'll check your leg on the way."

Markus was more than fine with Max flying after the creek ordeal. He seemed happy just to be on board his own ship and rummaged through a cupboard for an energy gel packet.

Kale's men stuck close together in a group. They looked tense, like they were waiting for something. Probably for orders from Kale to kill us all.

An engine rumbled in the distance just as we prepared for flight. We scrambled to the window to look out while Max jumped in Markus' pilot chair. The last Consulate ship rose in the distance over the area where we'd seen the laser blasts. Only the small lights on the wings of the ship were visible in the dark. I was glad we hadn't lifted off yet or we would have been spotted for sure. The Consulate ship hovered a minute on the other side of the creek, then rose even higher and took off at light speed.

"Where's it going?" Reed asked.

"Back to the Consulate, judging by the direction it's flying," said James. "Let's get over there and check on our people."

And the guns. What if they left because they killed the others and took all Dad's weapons? My stomach twisted at the thought. I also knew it hadn't escaped Kale that the last Consulate ship had left, meaning that any Consulate threat had disappeared. For now, at least. Whether they had the guns or not, the Consulate troops had left to regroup. Kale and his men were ship-less, and I doubted they planned to stay that way.

Max fired up the ship and it rose into the air. James grabbed his pack and walked over to Kale. "Might as well check that leg." He grabbed a vial and started to press it to Kale's leg. I didn't know what James was up to, but it had to be an act. It felt good to be on the other side of his acting this time.

Kale grabbed his hand firmly. "No pain meds. Just anti-biotics."

"Relax, that's what I'm giving you." James pressed the vial into the wound.

Kale jumped. "Saddam—fuckin'—Hitler!"

Sonya tried to hold his hand, but Kale shook her off. I couldn't remember which colors all the med vials were but hoped that whatever James was giving him was no antibiotic. Even if they were pain meds, it would help with whatever was coming next.

James brought out the electronic stitcher and closed up Kale's wound. Kale screamed some more names that I assumed were dictators before James quickly injected another vial into his leg. "Just to be safe," James said when Kale yelled again. "The wound looked pretty bad."

We were already landing by the time James zipped up his bag. Max brought the ship down in the clearing where Kale's ship had been. Markus opened the hatch, and I dashed out the door with James screaming at me to wait. I ran across the clearing. The rain had picked up again, going from a drizzle to a steady shower. I sloshed through huge puddles, and wished there was some moonlight for guidance. At least there wasn't fire to deal with. My toe caught on one of the guns and I fell to my knees. It was so quiet. No one else was around. Where was the Resistance if the guns were still here?

James reached me and waved to Max, who flipped on the ship lights. The piles of guns surrounded me. It didn't look like any were missing. Surely the Consulate would have taken them if they'd found them.

Kale, Sonya, and his men had joined us in the clearing. They stared from the guns to us and back again. Web, Trent, Bez, and Markus stood behind them, facing us. They looked ready to jump Kale and crew. My finger inched toward the trigger on my gun.

"James!" A man ran out from the woods, mud spraying out from his boots. "We thought it was another Consulate ship." He called out behind him, "It's safe."

Others came from the woods, a few of whom I recognized from the bar.

"Hey, Ollie. Good to see you guys," James said. "We saw the other ship take off."

"Yeah," one of the others said. "We got enough of their guys that I think they got scared off. It helped that they saw the other two ships crash and burn."

There were probably ten of them in all, which would be great if they were on our side. Not so great if they were with Kale.

Kale addressed the group in a loud voice. "Good work, soldiers. You sent those pansies running for their lives. They'll think twice before they mess with Kale Stark again." He stumbled in a puddle and caught himself. "I'm about done with this weather." Kale tried to bat the rain away with his gun.

I tilted my head toward James. "Pain meds?"

"Yep," he said.

"Not bad, soldier. Not bad at all," I whispered.

"We'll see." He smiled in the lights of the ship and spoke to me in a low voice. "Let's get these guns and get out of here, minus a few passengers."

James turned to the group by the woods. "We need to move these weapons before the Consulate comes back for them. Can you help us get them on board?"

"Sure, no problem," said Ollie. He motioned to the others, and they began taking armfuls of guns to the ship. Markus, Bez, and Web didn't move a muscle. I could tell they didn't want to turn their backs on Kale. The gun by my toe caught my attention. It would be helpful to have two guns again. I leaned down and casually picked it up.

"I'm going to check in with Markus and tell him the plan," I said, steering wide of Kale's group. Sonya eyed me and stepped in my direction.

"We'll help too," Kale's pilot said. He and another of Kale's men walked toward James and the weapons.

I froze, unsure what to do next.

James raised his gun at them. "That won't be necessary. We have this."

"What's with the lack of hospitality?" Kale asked, his words slurring together. "My men offered their assistance and that's how you treat them. Haven't I taught you better than that, soldier?"

My eyes were still focused on Kale's men when Markus yelled for me to watch out. Sonya whirled and had her arm around my neck and her gun pointed at my head. "You weren't thinking of leaving here without us, were you?" she asked, ice in her voice.

"Of course not," I said. "We just have to get the guns first."

She pressed her gun into my temple and wrenched mine from my hands. "Liar. And I know James didn't give him antibiotics either." She tossed the gun to Kale. Good thing the guns were still keyed to my vibration—and James'—or we'd all be dead.

I glanced up. Markus and James had their guns aimed at Sonya; Kale's men had their guns aimed at James; Web, Bez, and Trent had their weapons aimed at Kale; and Kale looked bewildered. If it stayed like this, it would be a blood-bath.

Sonya pressed my head downward with her weapon, right as a raindrop hit the center of a puddle underneath my feet.

I watched it splash onto the soaked ground.

Unless.

"Okay, you win," I said. "We'll take you all with us."

Kale laughed harshly. "I'm not sure we want to take you with us anymore, not with the way you've acted." He swayed, waving his gun around. "I've about had it with you, little Miss I-have-my-daddy's-guns-and-no-one-else-can-have-them. Fuck that."

He punched one of his men in the arm. "Let's do this already."

"James, shoot!" I yelled.

Kale's men opened fire and Sonya pushed the trigger button on the gun against my skull. The gun made a whirring sound but nothing happened. Sonya managed to say "Huh?" before she landed dead at my feet. The only laser that fired was from my dad's gun in James' hand, and it had hit Sonya square in the forehead. Kale and his men stared in disbelief at their guns and pressed the trigger buttons harder.

Markus shook his gun as he tried to get it to work.

"They're waterlogged," I yelled as James fired and took down two more of Kale's men, saying a mental thank-you to Dad. I don't know how he'd managed to test that out with the limited water supply on Earth but his hours of experimenting in his study totally paid off.

Markus shrugged and tossed his gun. He turned toward Kale, but Kale's pilot jumped on him from behind. Markus threw him down and they exchanged punches, and Bez and Trent joined in the pile, while I fished Trigger from my waistband and frantically worked to untangle her from the drawstring. I powered her up and aimed at the last of Kale's men, who had moved away toward the perimeter. Right as I fired at him and took him down, a knife whizzed by me and hit James.

I screamed and ran to him. Blood oozed from the side of his chest where the knife was embedded. Kale would have hit his heart if not for the med overdose.

In my peripheral vision, I saw Kale scoop up the super-weapon that Sonya had tossed to him and run into the woods. He must have had the knife in his pant leg. James pushed his weapon into my hand and stared into the trees. "Get him," he said, breathing heavily. "You can't let him get away with those guns."

Markus and Web ran toward us as Markus shouted. "Go, Tora! We've got James. Our guns won't work, but you can take him down. Get that burner for me."

I raced into the woods but felt ill about leaving James. How was I supposed to find Kale in the dark? He might be injured and doped up, but he still had the ability to hit James with a knife from a distance. Hopefully, that had been the only knife he had.

The woods were even darker than the clearing and the ground was just as muddy. Other than the light rain splattering the leaves, there was silence. A faint smoky smell lingered in the air from the fire but the trees here remained unscathed. I ran about twenty paces then stopped to listen. I'd been faster than him earlier when we'd run from the fire and crossed the creek. The pain meds might help him ignore the pain, but he'd still swayed and stumbled in the clearing.

If only my ankle would hold.

A crunch of leaves came from somewhere to my right. *Please let that be Kale and not a meat monster.* I tried to keep my breathing as quiet as possible. There it was. Another light crunch of leaves. I stepped carefully in the direction of the noise and kept my guns raised, Trigger in one hand, James' gun in the other.

Kale took off again, a rapid succession of twigs breaking as he ran. I went after him, no longer trying to mask the sounds of my running.

"That you, Tora?" he called out. "You're no match for me, with or without a gun."

"Then why are you running?" I shouted back.

He didn't answer. His footsteps got louder and I knew I was gaining ground on him. I ignored the branches that scraped my arms and face. One branch caught my hair and I cursed softly under my breath. I reached up and tore my hair from the tree before moving on. A minute later, the footsteps ceased.

Maybe Kale was tired and thought he'd hide. I took another step. The sound of his ragged breathing broke the silence of the forest. My own breath came in jagged bursts, and I'm sure he could hear me as well as I heard him. His breathing turned into a chuckle. I aimed Trigger where I thought he was and fired. Lasers lit up a tree and everything went dark again.

I listened for his breathing and he launched himself at me. His body flew into mine, knocking us both to the ground. James' gun flew out of my left hand. Kale had me pinned underneath him in the mud and his hands closed around my neck. He must have left Dad's super-gun in the trees. My right hand held Trigger but it was pinned under my own leg and the weight of Kale's body. I tried to wiggle my hand free but it wouldn't budge, so I punched at his arm with my left hand. His laughter told me my blows had no effect and he tightened his grip around my neck.

Things started to go black and I saw spots behind my eyes. I couldn't die like this. Not with James down. With my whole family dead. With Kale getting away with Dad's weapons. It had to end here.

"Think you're so tough now, soldier?" Kale asked. "I'm not sure what I'll do without you and James to fire the guns, but I'm sure as hell safer without you two traitors." He shifted his weight to bear fully down on my neck.

My lungs screamed for air. The pressure around my throat was unbearable. I made one last attempt to yank Trigger out from under me. It moved a little but I couldn't entirely free my hand. Though Kale had shifted his weight, it wasn't enough. Everything faded. As my consciousness drained away, I pushed Trigger up at the highest angle I could manage against my thigh and fired through my own leg.

Kale screamed and rolled off of me. I couldn't get in enough air to scream myself, though the pain that tore through the laser blast in my leg was excruciating. Air rushed into my lungs and I gasped and rolled onto my side, clutching at my throat. My vision started to clear a few seconds later, but my focus was on inhaling and exhaling. Kale's yelling continued, and I tried to focus in the dark. At least I knew I'd hit him. If I had to shoot myself, I hoped I'd been able to turn Trigger enough that it would be a straight shot through him too.

I pushed my hand into the mud and tried to sit myself up. Searing pain shot through my right thigh. Hopefully I hadn't shot through a major artery, or I'd bleed out pretty fast. My leg wouldn't hold my weight when I tried to put pressure on it. There was no way I could stand. For all I knew, there wasn't much left to stand on. I couldn't think about that now.

Kale stopped screaming. It sounded like he was crawling away, his labored breathing punctuated only by the occasional curse word. Maybe I'd taken out a good part of his leg too.

I flipped over on my belly and bit my tongue to keep from screaming. The taste of my own blood nauseated me, but I dug my elbows into the mud and dragged myself toward Kale. The rain had almost stopped and a small sliver of moonlight came through the trees.

Kale's form moved about five yards in front of me. He called me names I'd never heard before but I was sure they weren't complimentary. He left a wide trail of blood behind him as he clawed at the ground in his effort to get away. He wasn't moving very fast.

My throat burned when I called out, "Where you goin', soldier?" I coughed hard into the ground. "I'm going to make sure you never kill anyone's father or girlfriend, again, you burner."

He turned around, a look of surprise on his face. With great effort, I gritted my teeth and brought Trigger up to aim at him. He tried to scramble faster on his hands and knees to get to the nearest tree, blood pouring out with every move. My finger hovered over the trigger panel when I saw the eyes.

Red eyes just beyond Kale in the trees. *Crap.* Alec had said they were attracted to blood, and between Kale and me, there was an overwhelming stench of the stuff in the air. Kale looked up as the meat monster pounced. He lifted his arm to shield himself and the animal tore into his arm. It came away with a chunk of Kale in its teeth and went back for more. Kale yelled at the animal while yet more blood drained from his arm. There was nothing that Kale deserved more than getting eaten alive by one of those things.

I should want to watch him get ripped to shreds. Enjoy it even. But I couldn't.

Kale stared at the monster as it growled and prepared to pounce again. I propped myself up on my elbows, aimed between Kale's eyes, and fired. The monster jumped back, looking around as though confused. I moved the gun to the right and fired again. It fell without a sound.

It was then that I noticed my own blood leaking from under me. I touched my leg and it was soaked. My head spun. I tried to look up and could just make out part of Alec's Weeping Boy constellation through the trees. Everything started to fade again and I put my head down, laying my cheek against the cool mud. I'd just rest for a minute and then I'd get back to the others. Besides, I'd earned a short break. I'd gotten rid of Kale and caught dinner. I rocked.

Chapter TWENTY

"JAMES," I CALLED OUT.

"Sshhh, you need to rest, sweetcakes." A hand held mine and I struggled to open my eyes.

The light was bright and I squinted as my eyes adjusted. "Markus?"

"Who else would it be?"

I tried to sit up and Markus moved to help me. He put his arm around my shoulders and shifted me until I sat on the edge of the cot. We were inside one of the huts. "Is this our camp?" I asked.

Markus nodded. Reed and Alec sat together on the other side of the tent, holding hands. "*Hola*, Tora," said Alec. "Good to see you awake."

"How long have I been out?" I asked.

Reed counted on her hands. "Five light breaks? Crap, I don't know. A day maybe."

My thigh was bandaged in thick layers of cloth. Pain meds must have been involved because aside from a dull throb, I didn't feel much. At least my leg was still there, which had to be a good sign.

"Did James do this?" I asked, running my hand over the bandage. "Is he okay? Who helped him?"

Markus laughed. "Yes, to the first two questions. As for the last, luckily, I've seen James in action enough as a medic that he was able to walk me through it."

Markus handed me some water. "After I fixed James up, Web and I went searching for you in the woods. We'd heard the lasers and hoped you'd gotten Kale." He shook his head. "The last thing I expected was to find you passed out in the mud with a dead guy and a meat monster. Thanks for that, by the way, it was delicious."

I smiled weakly. "Thought you'd appreciate it."

"Anyway, Web gathered the guns while I carried you back here. James wanted to fix you up himself, even though he wasn't in great shape. He's been sleeping ever since. Hut next door. Max is with him." Markus stood up and offered me his hand. "And I'm guessing you want to head over, so I'll help."

"Thanks." I took his hand and stood gingerly. Fresh pain went through my leg but nothing was going to keep me away from James. "By the way, what happened to Kale's pilot? Last I saw, you were rolling on the ground with him."

"He's taken care of." Markus flexed his bicep in an

exaggerated manner. "Turns out I don't need a gun with these babies."

Alec laughed. *"Muy valiente, amigo."*

Reed rested her head on Alec's shoulder. "I'm just glad we're all okay."

I smiled at Reed and Alec as I left, leaning on Markus. He helped me hobble to the next hut. "I really am glad you're okay," he said. "While you're visiting James, I'm going to go find you a stick you can use to help you walk."

"Thanks." I leaned against the hut flap and peered inside. Max sat next to James, an assortment of vials and gadgets near his side. "Hi, Max."

Max jumped up and came over. "Here, let me help you." He brought me over to the cot where James lay asleep. I winced as I sat down on the bed and straightened out my leg.

"I'll leave you with him a minute," Max said. "Just yell if you need anything."

He left and I turned to James. His breathing was soft but steady, and he had a large bandage across his chest. I ran my hand along the stubble on his cheek and leaned over to kiss him gently on the lips.

His eyes fluttered open. "I was hoping that was you and not Max."

I laughed. "I can't believe you're okay." I looked down at my leg. "Thanks for saving me . . . again."

James smiled. "Anytime. You saved us. We've got all the guns thanks to you."

I touched his chest lightly. "We look kind of cute in our matching bandages."

He pulled me to him, and I kissed him again until he coughed. I'd been pressing on his chest. "Oops, sorry."

James hacked into his arm. "Don't ever apologize for kissing me. Just give me a sec."

I ran my hand through his hair. "Get better fast, okay?"

James raised an eyebrow. "Why? Are you offering to do more than kiss me?"

A flush crept across my face. "Maybe, but I don't want to hurt you."

He laughed and coughed again. "You were pretty impressive. I'll try to heal quickly." A coughing fit overcame him and I tried to give him water, then called for Max when the cough didn't stop. "I think he might need something stronger," I said to Max.

Max grabbed a vial and pressed it to James' arm. "This will help. You need to rest a while more to heal that lung."

The coughing eased and James grabbed for my hand. I held it as he drifted off to sleep. "You're beautiful," he murmured as his eyes closed.

I sat there with his hand in mine.

Max sighed. "You can stay, but no more excitement until he's better. Got it?"

I blushed. "Got it."

Max sat by the door and leaned back against the hut wall. The exhaustion showed in his face, and I knew he was still healing from his own injury. His eyes shut after a bit.

I got more comfortable on the cot, careful not to disturb James, and let my thoughts drift. We couldn't stay here long, not now that the Consulate knew where we were. We'd have to move as soon as possible to a safer location. And somehow, along the way, I'd get rid of the guns once and for all.

James cried out in his sleep, and I stroked his hand until the pain passed.

Chapter TWENTY-ONE

Three Days Later

THE GUNS WERE SECURELY STORED ON MARKUS' SHIP AND we'd gathered all the final supplies. I hobbled around with the stick Markus had found for me, asking if anyone needed help. Though my leg felt stronger each day, I still needed some assistance with walking.

"Thanks, Gunner. We're good," one man responded to me.

After taking down the Consulate ships and shooting Kale, some of the Resistance started calling me "Gunner." It wasn't the sweetest term of endearment I'd heard, but at least they were on our side.

We'd head to Dais and hope that the colony there would welcome us with open arms. Or at least not shoot us on sight. Once the Consulate regrouped, they were sure to come back knowing that Dad's weapons were some-where within reach. Since nowhere on Caelia was out of their reach, it was decided that no one could remain—for the time being, anyway. The problem was that everyone wouldn't fit on Markus' ship, and it was all we had.

James, Max, Markus, Web, and I would go first, along with a few other Resistance members. Max figured that the new colony might be more receptive if we first brought James, a medic, with us, along with some supplies. If they allowed us to borrow one of their ships, then both Markus and Max could return for the rest of the group. Alec and Reed offered to stay behind with the others.

"I've heard one of the moons around Dais is made mostly of diamonds," Reed said, her hand twined through Alec's.

That got Markus' attention. "That sounds like an inter-esting business venture right there."

I shook my head.

"What?" Markus said. "I'm done with the gun busi-ness. Too violent, you know?"

James walked up behind me and wrapped his arms around my waist. "You ready?"

I smiled. "Ready as ever. I'm just sad to be leaving here. I'll really miss the beach."

He squeezed me. "You and me both."

I batted his arm. "That's not what I meant."

James and Markus carried the last few packs to the ship, though James wasn't supposed to carry anything heavier than a few pounds for several more months. I looked around Caelia one last time. Part of me would stay here, with Dad, with the ocean. I hated to leave the lush trees and the scent of the wildflowers, even if it was only for a little while. To go from a pod city and an underground bunker to a place like this was unbelievable.

I don't think I ever really believed I'd make it off Earth. I thought I was destined to die on that sun-scorched, water-challenged planet, yet here I was on Caelia. Which made it that much harder to leave.

Alec jogged up to me with barely a limp in his step. "Here," he said. He had a pink flower in his hand and slid it behind my ear. "To remember us until we're all together again."

I fingered the soft petals. "Thanks, but I'll see you soon enough." I glanced over at Reed. "I'm glad you two found each other. She's a sweetheart."

Alec nodded. "Yeah, she is. Take care of yourself, Tora." He leaned over. "And don't tell, but I'll always consider you my *ángel*."

I smiled. "It's our secret. And a way better a nickname than Gunner, for sure."

I looked over at the ship and knew it was time to get on board. The light break had brought a soft, warm wind and the sky was a crystal clear blue. It boded well for a good flight. My friends that were staying behind seemed content, and those going with me were optimistic. Everyone was on the mend and I knew that the days I'd need a walking stick were limited. A slight queasiness lingered in my belly but I knew it was it was due to having to leave Caelia.

A wave of nostalgia hit me as Markus' ship rose into the air. I might be leaving for now, but Callie City was my home and those Consulate burners weren't going to keep me away for long. When they came back and found Callie City deserted and the weapons gone, that would be the end of it. They'd go back to their side of the planet and hopefully never set foot here again. I was taking back my city, my beach, and my flowers as soon as possible. The ocean with its pink sand beach was the last thing I saw as we zipped away toward the horizon through the calm skies.

"I'll be back," I whispered to the waves below.

Acknowledgments

I'VE HEARD SEQUELS ARE TRICKY, BUT THIS BOOK WAS A BLAST to write, and I'm so thankful for the people that helped me along the way. A huge thanks to my fearless agent, Jessica Regel, for her insights and comments, which make me a better writer, and for her all-around awesomeness. Also, thanks to JVNLA, especially Laura Biagi, who gave me fantastic notes on this book, as well as Jennifer Weltz and Tara Hart, whose tweets always make me smile. I'm so grateful to everyone at Egmont USA, especially my fantastic editor, Alison Weiss, for believing in this series. This book would not be what it is without my phenomenal beta readers: Valerie Kemp (a.k.a. the plot-hole queen), Lynne "Zloty" Matson, and Sara Raasch ("young Sara"). I'd have lost my sanity entirely without the support of the incredible YA Valentines, and my amazing writer friends, Wendy Terrien, Sue Duff, and Aimee Henley.

I feel so lucky to have people shouting about this series to the world, including Michelle Bayuk and Margaret Coffee at Egmont, and the awesome team of Julie Schoerke, Sami Jo Lien, Marissa DeCuir Curnette, and Grace Wright at JKS Communications. The science in this book was vastly improved thanks to Fran Bagenal, Professor of Astrophysical and Planetary Sciences at the University of Colorado-Boulder. Any scientific errors are entirely mine.

Finally, to all my friends (both online and in the real world) and my family, thanks so much for your love and support. To my hubby and kiddos, you're my everything and make me feel like the luckiest person on this little planet. Thank you.